# RUE FRENCH
# MUST DIE

*Lew McKimmon, 2014*

Contributing Editor N. Keene
Cover Photo Sarah Lang Photography
Consultant Scott Turner

ISBN: 0989773817
ISBN 13: 9780989773812
Library of Congress Control Number: 2014915187
Lew McKimmon Books, Indianapolis, Indiana

# CHAPTER ONE

Early October, 1866, on a farm in Northern Virginia

The lovely dark-haired girl walked softly among the flowers in the formal garden which lay hidden behind her family home, enjoying the fragrance of the day, while humming a tune that her mother had taught her long, long ago. Folks said she was her mother over---her gentle laugh, warm smile, and joyful manner making for an easy comparison. Her recently washed hair, long and dark, would dry quickly in the light autumn breeze, which stayed busy scattering those few leaves which had already chosen to fall, anxious to be first in the beautiful parade of color which filled these northern Virginia hills year after year.

Ginny Stronton had been to this place of beauty before, back when it was still the home of the family O'Dell, and of the last of their line, Catherine. But she had known Catherine for only a day or two, in a desperate and painful time, when both had been held as captive, with the threat of death always near.

Catherine had managed to escape, and had fled far to the west, running from the evil of her wicked step-uncle, and his passion for killing. Ginny had not been so fortunate. Instead, she was taken away to be used as chattel, to be treated as the white slave she had become.

But her prayers were answered, and Ginny's father, a General, and a gentleman, had found her at last, rescuing her away from that den of thieves. He then dealt harshly with those who had preyed upon her, cleansing the land of their filth, and rescuing other girls from their imprisonment as well.

From now on they would live here on this beautiful estate given to them by that same Catherine O'Dell, a gift of love and of hope: love for the home where she had grown up happy and free, and hope for a man who was looking for his long lost daughter. It was a gift which gave peace to the giver as much as it did to the given.

This place of flowers was Ginny's home now, two stories of painted white with green shutters, two wings for bedrooms, and a wide covered porch, perfect for entertaining or the occasional afternoon luncheon. Ginny was enveloped by the fragrance of the place, fresh and green, with late summer flowers still blooming. She herself was as lovely as any of the flowers the garden could boast. She belonged in this place, this sanctuary. Here she could live and flourish and heal.

Her big chestnut horse was already saddled and waiting when she got down to the stables. The horse was as happy to be off and running as was the girl, anticipating the joy of wind flowing through their unkempt manes, and tasting the free and open air surrounding them--- a means of escape from the confinement and aloneness of solitude.

But Ginny's daily rides of joy would not last. She did not yet know that the evil which had once stolen her away from her happiness and her home had somehow survived her father's terrible vengeance. The peace would soon be broken, as a specter from her unhappy past sped down upon her from the north. Evil still lived in the form of a man, and it would find her once again. He brought with him the power to open wounds not yet healed, and to touch her more intimately than mere flesh could ever make itself known.

Later that same night, and hundreds of miles to the north, the lonely whistle of the southbound train to Philadelphia could be heard drifting across the Pennsylvania country side, the engine's metal clad form appearing like a phantom under the moon lit sky. Passengers were few on this trip, and were as nondescript as most such travelers would tend to be at this time of night. Excepting for one. One stood out, being very different from the others.

That one exception was the well-dressed man sitting alone in the fourth seat of the second passenger car. He was not sleeping, or reading, or staring out the window to take in the damp gray autumn landscape which glistened under the full moon above. Instead, he sat motionless, focusing only on his immediate surroundings. He had spoken to no one. His life depended on it.

He was a handsome fellow with dark hair neatly trimmed, and intense brown eyes that seemed to peer deep into a man's soul. His blocked brown hat, green velvet vest, brass button overcoat, fitted gray pants, and polished boots would make this man stand out in any crowd. He was a man who always dressed well, and in the latest style, knowing that this gave him an advantage, with men, with women, and with his brand of success. And he was very successful.

No one seemed to know his name, at least not his real name. And yet, he was a man of many names, and many identities, chosen as needed, with no more concern than choosing a seat in a restaurant. Still, he was always careful about that sort of thing--- always sitting near the back, where he could easily see those who came and went, friend and foe alike. Or even a prospect for easy pickings.

He was a professional liar who used his skills as a swindler, a thief, a pretender, and impostor to his best advantage. He could change occupations as easily as other men changed shirts, posing as anything from a government official, to a doctor, to a clergyman, and more, as the circumstances required, and always at a profit. But truth be known, he had only one career--that of being a very skillful and dangerous man.

He needed a shave, and disliked the feel of his four day old beard as it itched on his face. He made a point of always being clean shaven, and longed to visit a barber. But he knew he could not enjoy the luxury of a close shave and a hot towel this day. He couldn't take the chance of being seen out in the open, especially in a place so busy and visible from the street as a barber shop. For on this night, and for several nights before, the hunter had become the hunted. He was on the run. His friends were out to kill him.

Of course, a man in his profession has no friends, no true friends that is, only those he was confident in doing business with---and even then only at a distance. But his business had recently become far more deadly. In the last four days he had killed three men, two he knew, one he didn't. Each of them had come gunning for him. They had been too slow, or too careless, or too confident---and they had died. None had lived long enough to tell him why, or who had given the order for his death. He figured it could only be the work of one man---McPhearson.

Jacob McPhearson--- just his name sent chilblains down the spine of any man who would dare to cross him. His reputation with his gun, with his knife, and his obsession with cruelty, went unmatched. It was McPhearson who had brought him along into his organization as an enforcer, a front man, and a fellow swindler. Jacob McPhearson had become wealthy trading in opium, armed robbery, black-mail, and slavery, especially white slavery---the kidnapping of young white girls from the frontier and shipping them to points unknown, often overseas. The demand was high, the supply was plentiful, and their disappearance was easily blamed on the Indians.

And so he was forced now to head south, out of New York, and down to Virginia, down to Jacob's recently embezzled farm. The matter of this death mark demanded that the account be settled, most likely with an exchange of lead in lieu of gold. This was the currency both men knew all too well, spent as needed, and never in short supply.

So far in these last few days he had been lucky, or good, or both. But the good die young, while the lucky live to fight another day. His thoughts had drifted back again to the pretty young woman sitting just a few seats in front of him. He had to admit, it had been a long time since he...

Suddenly, behind him, there was a voice, soft spoken and menacing, and the click of a revolver placed against his neck. His luck had run out.

"Rue French, my good friend. You've gotten careless in your old age. And now, thanks to you, I'm going to be a very wealthy man."

It looked as though Rue French's journey through life was about to come to a sudden and painful end. No man can dodge the devil forever.

French knew the voice, and he knew the gun, a Colt, and a well-used one if he was right about the voice---and he was. This was Bo Findley.

Six foot, two, thin build, curly dark hair, and a hat that had seen better days, Findley was known for his stealth, his skill, and his viciousness. The well-dressed man he had called Rue French didn't need to see Findley's face to know who he was, or to know that he had come to kill him.

He knew that Findley was one of the best, and that he had only one weakness---he was a lousy shot. But that wasn't going to help this day, not with the Colt's barrel resting there just below his ear. This hand was dealt, and Findley held all the aces. The notorious Rue French was as good as dead.

But not yet. In fact, French was better than dead, he was still alive, and fully intended to be still alive long after Bo Findley lay still and dead in his place. French was determined to play out the hand.

Bo liked to talk, and he liked to hear his victims talk-- to hear the anxious fear in their voices, to see the sweat run down their necks as they saw the glowing specter of death staring at them with no hope of mercy, no way out.

There had been only three other people in that rail car as it left New York for Philadelphia. As far as French knew, they were still seated exactly where they had been when they left. There was an old man, bundled up and sleeping with his head under his hat, a spinster, sitting straight and proper like, and trying to read a book in the dim light the smoking oil lamps provided, and a younger woman, in her twenties from the looks of her, sitting just a few seats in front of him, admittedly the source of guilty distraction which had assisted Findley in his work. A quick glance told the tale---the old man was gone! Findley's disguise had been perfect. The fox had been bested by the weasel.

Rue French was not his real name. In fact, of all the names he had hung upon himself to do his bidding, Rue French was not among them. That name had been curiously assigned to him after he had handed a former co-conspirator participating in a bank heist a note saying where they should meet---in this case French Street, Rue being the French word for street. The reader of the note mistook the meaning of the words and ended up somewhere else. But from then on it was how he would be known, and as he never used his own name, the moniker stuck.

This man that Findley knew as Rue French had no qualms about killing. He had done it often enough, and in whatever manner the circumstances called for---hands, knives, guns, and even poisoned drinks from time to time. But he never killed for fun, only business. This encounter with Findley was simply the business they were in.

That young woman sitting in front of them was in line for any bullet that French would dodge as it came spewing from Findley's gun. He would have tried it, he would have turned quickly and grappled with Findley, hoping that the shot would go wide and offer a chance for survival. But Rue French had never killed a woman, and he had no intention of getting one killed today just to save his own worthless skin. But then, Bo Findley's skin wasn't worth saving either. The matter was decided--- he needed to change the game, if not the outcome.

"Alright, Bo, you win. But not here, not where these people could get hurt. That's not our way, and you know it. I'll speak up, and tell them that you're robbing me, and that they should stay put or they'll get hurt. Then we'll walk out that door up there and you can do what you came to do. It's the only way." French knew that Findley was ruthless, but that he suffered from a lack of imagination. He was counting on it.

"Sure French, sure. Whatever makes you feel better. Then after I'm done with you I'll rob them anyway. They'll give me anything I want after they seen what I done to you." Findley had taken the bait.

The two men walked slowly to the end of the swaying rail car, Findley's Colt still nuzzling French's neck while the astonished passengers watched in horror as French spoke, gun to his head.

"This man is a thief and a robber. Do as he says and you won't be harmed. But first, as you can see, he and I have a little personal business to tend to." Findley didn't much like that speech, and hadn't really seen the need for all this play acting in the first place. But he was more than happy to go along if it meant taking Rue French off guard and without a fight. French was known as a very dangerous man, the worst of a bad lot. Findley couldn't believe his luck.

The coach door opened, and the men slowly passed through, the drama clearly visible through the glass. As the door came shut, the gun sounded, and Rue French disappeared from sight.

Bo Findley was still relishing in his good fortune as French walked through the door without resistance. He was fully expecting some sort of foolishness---a struggle, a plea for mercy, an attempt to buy his way out of it, something. But French hadn't said a word in his own defense, only a plea on behalf of the others riding in the rail car with him.

But just as Findley pulled the car door shut, his world suddenly came apart, and everything went wrong. At the very instant the door closed French heaved his powerful frame against the unsuspecting Findley, causing both men to fall freely over the safety chain, and down into the darkness of the Pennsylvania foothills below.

Findley's gun went off, but with no purpose, its target becoming lost in the forty foot free-fall which followed, the two killers grappling in a deadly dance, plunging downward into the rock strewn crevasse below. Death awaited them there with open arms.

At the last second, and by the thinnest of margins, French grabbed the falling Findley, clutching his shirt, and pulled him up close. The impact was sudden and final, flesh against rock, a contest as one sided as death itself.

The night train thundered on with no regard for the missing men. The other passengers quickly found the conductor, telling him their stories of terror, and of the unfortunate man, who having protected them, had disappeared into the darkness of the night.

Nothing could be done until the train reached the station. The authorities were notified, and a search party would return at first light. But no sign of either man would ever be found along the tracks, or in the surrounding countryside.

The missing men's tickets had already been punched, their final destinations long ago determined.

No artist could have painted a more beautiful morning. Recent rains splashed and played over smooth boulders which had long ago tumbled into the creek bed below. Dark green leaves fluttered in the breeze, accompanied by a chorus of songbirds cheerfully bringing in the day. The sun painted the sky in pinks and yellows in an ever-changing display of nature's splendor.

But the specter which greeted Rue French this morning was far more ghastly than beautiful, a thing to be forgotten, and not for the faint of heart. There below him was Bo Findley's discolored face, looking up at the lovely morning sky with lifeless eyes, his expression still seeming to ponder the perfect caper gone wrong, all that money waiting for him right there, just out of reach--forever.

Rue French had seen dead men before, and had often enough been the one who had made them that way. Seeing Bo's dead body wasn't a matter for concern. It was more the unsettling realization that he had spent the night sprawled across that man's lifeless corpse that caused the bile to rise in his throat. Bo had never been a handsome fellow, and laying broken and lifeless upon that unyielding rock as he was, did nothing to improve his looks.

But Bo had done French a favor by taking the brunt of their forty foot fall from that train car the night before, and leaving his would-be victim with little more than a bruise and a scrape or two. And so, given the circumstances, Rue French could only consider Findley's lifeless form to be a thing of beauty, a lifesaving cushion from the fall, an unintended gift of life bestowed among thieves, as it were.

French stood on wobbly legs and assessed his luck. The train had been within a few miles of Philadelphia when Bo had stuck the barrel of the Colt to his neck. This creek, like most all creeks, surely ran to a river, which ran to the sea, so finding his way wouldn't be all that difficult. He could of course climb back up to the rails and follow them into the city, but he figured that after what all had happened on and off the train the night before, his appearance might be difficult to explain.

Somehow his pistol had remained in his shoulder holster, and except for the dirt and moss stains on his clothing, he was pretty much intact. Bo had even been thoughtful enough not to bleed on his suit coat. No doubt the fall onto the boulder had broken Bo's back, or his neck, or both. Whatever had killed him, it had been quick.

The bag! French's carpet bag had been sitting beside him on the bench there in the passenger car. In it he kept extra clothes, weapons, papers, and money, lots of money, all now left behind, the profits from months of thievery gone in seconds. Someone else now no doubt was enjoying the spoils of his talents. He swore bitterly at the loss.

French knew he'd been dealt a lousy hand. People he had once known as partners were now out to kill him. It was apparent that there was a price on his head, and a substantial price it must be, considering how determined his would-be assassins had been in coming after him these last many days. He recalled now his reason for being on that train heading south, a train that he had been forced to abandon in a most unacceptable manner --- McPhearson. This was a score that needed to be settled, and the sooner the better.

But there was no profit in standing around admiring Bo's lifeless carcass. He needed to get moving and away from there. But just as Bo's demise had worked to French's advantage, having his body laying out there in the open like that could also spell his doom, especially as his own body would be nowhere nearby to be found as well. Better none than one. Grabbing Findley's arms, French dragged the lifeless corpse to a nearby ravine, carefully covering him with fallen timbers and brush, visible now to only the most ardent of searchers.

Rue French then washed his hands in the stream, and straightening his clothes, resumed his journey, on foot for now, but determined to reach his goal. He was stiff and sore from this latest ordeal, but set off with purpose in his step, a loaded pistol in his holster, and sweet vengeance burning in his heart.

# CHAPTER TWO

General Henry James Stronton, late of the Army of Virginia, sat regally on his splendid gray horse, enjoying the cool morning air, and taking in the beauty of this place he now called home. Rustling leaves signaled the coming of autumn, as season again followed season, year after year.

This estate had been the home of the O'Dells, a family rich in history and tradition, who had loved this land and worked it with skilled hands from generation to generation. But tragedy had befallen this noble family, along with its last remaining child, Catherine O'Dell. She had been forced to flee the evil that had infested this place of happiness, seeking shelter in the unknown lands to the west.

It was Catherine who, upon hearing of Stronton's quest to find his lost daughter, Ginny, gave deed to this beautiful farm as a gift to celebrate the reunion of father and daughter yet to come, with a chance to somehow leave a legacy of permanence to a home she knew she would never return to.

Stronton gazed thoughtfully over toward the O'Dell family gravesite, and to the newly hewn headstone honoring William O'Dell, Catherine's father. He had fallen at the battle of Shiloh, and was buried there that day along with hundreds of his comrades, in a place now known only to God. This headstone did not mark the man's final resting place, but rather his loving memory, and his sacrifice.

The General was a man who kept his promises. Upon accepting Catherine's generous gift, he promised to watch over the graves of her family, and to put up a marker for her fallen father. A military salute had accompanied the setting of the stone, a solemn moment, a cherished life remembered.

But Catherine O'Dell gave Stronton a far more precious gift than this beautiful farm---she had given him his daughter. It was Catherine who told the General about the inner workings of the den of evil which had taken his daughter Ginny into the world of white slavery where she was held as captive. It was Catherine's suggestion that he impersonate the notorious killer Rue French, in order to infiltrate that organization, and to somehow locate and rescue the girl.

The plan had worked perfectly. Ginny was home once again, home now in this wonderful place of flowers and forests and crisp morning air. The stench of the man named Jacob McPhearson, mastermind of that ring of evil, the man who had stolen the O'Dell family farm from its rightful heir, was now gone, forever. His worthless carcass lay dead and buried deep in southwest Kansas soil, a victim of his own brand of cruelty.

Stronton took one last look at William's stone, the nearby flowers bending softly in the gentle breeze, and saluted his fallen comrade with a prayer of thanks. Here then was a kinship as strong as blood itself.

To secure the memory of the O'Dell family, and of its years of stewardship to the land, Stronton had given this estate a new name, a name which would last for generations to come. It was Christened 'Dellmont', a name which honored both the O'Dell legacy, and the nearby mountains which had stood as silent guardians over this place since time unknown.

Dellmont. The name was a fitting tribute, the gesture a matter of honor.

For a man like Rue French, stealing a horse wasn't a problem. Stealing a horse that was a hard runner and didn't attract attention was the problem. There wasn't much riding stock to be had down by the Philadelphia waterfront that night, and most of what was there, was either ready for glue or stolen from someone living nearby---a horse not likely to go unnoticed.

They were out to get him, so the train station would be watched, as would the livery barns, and the passenger ferries as well. A man would think that it would be easy to disappear in a town the size of Philadelphia, what with so many people around and all. That was usually the case. But not on this day, and not for this man.

Rue French stood six feet two in his bare feet, and sporting a frighteningly handsome face and strong athletic build, he stood out in a crowd, anywhere, any time. While he had passed himself off with any number of assumed names, and pretended to practice any number of respected professions as the circumstance demanded, he was not a man who was easily forgotten. It was a liability, especially now.

French never gambled, stayed out of dance halls, and never took a drink from a stranger, or anyone else for that matter. But the men who were out for his scalp would be well known in such places, making them off limits as he considered where he could hide unseen and unnoticed. Now, for the first time in his life, it was he who was being stalked, and he didn't like it one bit. Jacob McPhearson! Only he would have the nerve to order these attempts on his life. But why? Business had dropped a bit now that the war was over, but there was always money to be made in the opium trade, and the running of white slaves, always chancy at best, remained a ready market among the kings of the desert. And although French had no direct dealings in the kidnapping of young women, he'd done nothing to interfere with that practice which he considered to be "ungentlemanly". Smuggling had always been a matter of much risk for much reward. There were always a few trusted sea captains who would transport a special cargo or two as needed, if the price was right.

But tonight French couldn't trust them either. No man or woman for that matter could be trusted, whether he knew them or not. He needed to get to McPhearson and fast, if he was going to save his hide. And if Jacob admitted to putting out this contract on him, so be it. At least French would know who to shoot next.

Mounting a likely looking gelding with good lines but questionable origins, French rode south, eager to get out of town as quickly as possible. The horse didn't seem to object. A good horse and a good road are a blessing to any traveler, especially one on the run. At least he had chosen a good horse. The road needed work.

Rue French was running from his enemies, from his friends, from the unseen and the unknown. But his greatest enemy was time. If the price on his head was as great as he feared it might be, he would attract the best among those who killed for a living. Massed together they would be a force far greater than he could overcome alone, and he knew he could count on no one to come to his aid. Those who would gladly sell their own mother would not hesitate to sell him out as well.

The full moon remained hidden behind the clouds, the darkness of the night becoming his friend, a place where he could hide unnoticed as he traveled south. The darkness of the night was also his enemy, a place where those who hunted him could lie unseen in ambush. He rode on.

# CHAPTER THREE

Rue French wasn't his real name. Neither was James Tower, Cedric Randal, Peter Fisher, or Christian Henderson, or a half dozen other names for that matter. He wore names like other men wore hats. He could speak like a native from just about any part of the country, throwing in a little Spanish and French as well when needed. These skills had served him well before, and he intended to use them again, and soon. But first he needed a change of clothes, and a change of scenery. He coaxed his stolen mount along a little faster.

While he was pleased to have encountered no problems leaving Philadelphia, his mind dwelt on the carpet bag that he had been forced to leave behind on the train from New York, back where Bo Findley had made his move. The carpet bag would remain safe on board until someone looked inside and found a goodly stash of money and other stolen valuables. It was not a thing that French could calmly go back to the next station to inquire about.

In the bag were his shaving kit, an extra pistol, spare cartridges, two changes of clothes, and money, lots of money. All these things were easily enough replaced, including the money. But that took time, and planning, and a man on the run, and in this case running from his own people, was short on both. Right now he needed that bag.

French didn't know the area south of Philadelphia all that well, but he did know people. The further out he got from civilization, the fewer chances he could take. Most folks would figure it to be the other way around, but the truth was that a thief could more easily hide and operate in a city with all its people and shadows than out in the sticks where everybody knew everybody else and their cousins and their business. But by now French was wondering if he would be able to hide anywhere.

It was getting near dark when he approached a humble looking house about a mile off the main road. He straightened his tie and sat upright on his stolen mount. Tonight Rue French would pass himself off as Christian Henderson, a lawyer, looking for a meal and place to stay the night. It was one of his most convincing roles.

He rode on in.

French approached the darkened house as though he expected to meet a hungry bear at any moment. His gun was not drawn, but it was always at the ready, and his eyes searched everywhere. It was nearly dark, but there was no lamp lit inside the house that he could tell, and no smoke from the chimney. The place seemed lifeless and abandoned.

But French hadn't lived this long counting on how things seemed.  The stolen horse had handled well, good breeding no doubt, and obediently turned back to where the barn and an adjacent corral stood dark and empty like the rest of the place.  He expected to maybe hear a horse sound coming from inside the barn, but at the same time, he didn't.  There was no fresh smell of stock here, no sign of use.  Nothing.

Against his better judgment, French went ahead and dismounted, tying off the horse on a ring just outside the barn door.  He was tired of sitting anyway as that saddle had been made for a man much smaller than him.  He stopped near the doorway of the barn, just off to one side so as not to cast a silhouette of himself against the evening sky.  He stood very still and listened with his eyes closed.  Nothing.

He stepped on inside the barn and pulled his sidearm with his right hand while lighting a match with his left, holding the flame far away from his body.  Nothing.  He found a coal oil lamp on a peg just inside the door, right where he knew it would be.  Looking around, it only took a minute or so to confirm what he already knew--there had been no one in that barn for some time.

Most men would have assumed then and there that the place was deserted, and gone right on over and into the house.  Rue French knew better.  He located a pitch fork, and hanging the lantern on the tines, walked carefully over to the house with the lantern down and away from him.  He wasn't being overly cautious, he didn't believe there was such a thing.  Somehow he hadn't noticed earlier that the front door to the house was slightly ajar.  A man could be hiding behind that door waiting with a rifle, or worse, a shotgun.  He changed his angle of approach so that any would-be gunman would have to open the door wider to maintain his target, thus giving himself away. There was an overhang above the door which reflected the lantern's light as he approached. He needed to know who or what was inside, but he knew that finding out too quickly could prove to be the last thing he'd ever do. He took his time.

French used the pitchfork to slowly push the door open, the attached lantern lighting the way. There was a small table, with a cloth, and two chairs tucked carefully in. It was all nice and neat. He pushed the door open the rest of the way and cautiously peered inside.

Suddenly a familiar odor filled the air, but mixed with something else---something... He pulled the lantern back, but it was too late.

The lantern caught the fumes, and the explosion which followed blew the house apart, lifting it off its foundation, and hovering in the air for the briefest of seconds, returning it to the earth in a cascade of wood and soil, burying Rue French along with his alias in a four-foot pile of shredded timbers.

The explosion was heard for miles around, rumbling like thunder through the hills and back again. This sort of thing had been happening more and more often lately, and folks out that way no longer gave much mind to it. They had heard it all before.

Just down the road about a mile or so, Zachariah Shartle and his son, Gabe, had just put the horses up for the night and were headed in to supper when the unnerving boom of the explosion ripped through the air and shook itself back and forth in the nearby hills.

"Third one this month. You'd think it would have blowed itself out by now. I told them they should have never capped the mine off like that. That sounded like it came from down toward old man Trotter's place. I'm not surprised. It's been stinkin' down that way for weeks now."

Shartle stopped and looked down toward the direction of the Trotter farm. There were no flames on the horizon to be seen. He figured maybe the recent rains had soaked everything up to the point nothing could catch fire anyway.

"We'll go on down there in the morning and see if anything needs done. Probably not, but we'll go down and see anyway." They went on in to supper.

# CHAPTER FOUR

"Over here, Pa!" Zachariah and his son had ridden over to old man Trotter's place the next morning after breakfast had been eaten and the chores were finished. They were more curious to see what might be left of the place than thinking they might be looking for survivors. Old Trotter and his wife hadn't been seen in months, and most folks figured they had just up and left to go live with his brother in Ohio. Trotter never much talked to anybody anyhow, and folks not knowing where he had got off to was something that fit right in to his ways.

But the boy had come across something that didn't belong there --- a horse, tied up at the corner of the barn and hiding just inside the doorway. The barn had remained pretty much intact during the explosion.

But the house told a different story. It had always been a pretty little place, with a vegetable garden on the south exposure, and flowers of all sorts planted around. The Trotters kept to themselves whenever possible, but were always polite if not friendly to folks who came by. After the mine was closed down, the gases coming up through the vents gave the place a terrible smell from time to time, and killed off most of the flowering plants. It made it hard just to breathe some days.

Zachariah knew full well that Trotter didn't have a saddle horse, especially one as fine as this. Seeing that the horse had been wearing its saddle for some time, and was in need of water, he figured that whoever had ridden in on it was more than likely still around, very possibly under the pile of rubble that had once been a house. Zachariah went on over to look around while the boy sensibly went to taking care of the horse.

Sifting through the shattered remains of the structure, Zach almost immediately came across a body, but not of anyone who had ridden in on that horse. It was old man Trotter himself, dead for some time now it seemed, all dried up as he was. A few feet away he found the man's wife, her body in pretty much the same condition, wearing what was left of her night shirt. He'd need to be getting the Sheriff out here to deal with all of this, as there would surely be an inquest into their deaths.

As he turned to walk back over to the barn, he heard a man's voice moan behind him. Zachariah aged ten years on the spot and turned white as a sheet, fearing that Trotter's ghost was coming after him. The boy had heard it as well, and came over at once, thinking his father had been hurt. Then the voice moaned again. The source of the sound was coming out from under the front door, now laid flat, and covered over by a stack of shingles.

It took a few minutes work, but soon enough the door was lifted off, and beneath it lay a man dressed in what had once been fine clothes, now torn and bloodied, with a pitchfork clutched in his hand. The man seemed barely alive, and the boy was sent back home after the wagon. Zachariah knelt beside the man and offered him water from the canteen that he always kept on his pommel.

"What's your name, mister?" Zachariah had been through the war, and knew it was important to get the injured man to drinking water and talking if possible. He repeated, "What's your name?" The man lay there, looking into his rescuer's eyes, seemingly looking for something he couldn't find somehow.

"I don't know." And taking a drink, he slid off into darkness.

Rue French woke up hours later in an unfamiliar room, surrounded by unfamiliar faces. His instinct was to reach for his pistol, but seeing the badge on the man standing in the corner, he knew it wouldn't be where he left it.

He remembered the blast, and the smell of coal gas just before that. He also remembered being buried by an enormous weight, under which he could breathe, but he couldn't move. He didn't remember much else.

But he did recall someone asking him his name, and that he'd done a good job of saying nothing, acting like he didn't know. Rue French wasn't really suffering from amnesia, but he had used that ruse more than once to stall for time to get out of a fix. He was just playing possum, kinda like anyway.

Truth was, at that point in time, it really didn't matter. Were they intending to pile the wood back atop of him if they didn't like his answer? Most likely not. He'd wait and play the amnesia act for as long as necessary and see just who they thought he was.

"Well, I see you're coming around. That's a nasty little bump you have on your head, my friend. But other than a swollen ankle, you seem to have come through it all in one piece." French assumed that the speaker was the local Doctor, what with his vested suit and stethoscope hanging from his neck. The fellow in the corner with the badge was most likely the local Sheriff, but the man in the doorway was unknown--maybe his rescuer. The girl sitting in the chair to French's left strongly resembled the Doctor, excepting that she was quite a bit prettier and had no mustache. The Sheriff came forward.

"First off mister, I'm Sheriff Samuel Hoskins, and you're under arrest. Second of all, there's the matter of who you are, and what you were doing at the Trotter place. Third, after searching your clothes, it seems that your name is either Henderson, Tower, Fisher, Randal, or who knows what. Do any of these names sound familiar to you?" Hoskins knew what all those name cards were most likely used for, and had a good idea as to the kind of man he was dealing with here.

"I'm sorry. None of those names sound familiar to me. I wish I could be more helpful." French would continue to play the only card he had left at the moment, amnesia. He had been in worse spots before, and this Sheriff didn't seem like much of an obstacle.

"Very well. You will remain here under house arrest until you are well enough to travel, and I can take you up to the jail. Maybe by then you'll get your memory back. Then you'll give me some answers about the two bodies we found in the rubble of that house, both of whom were murdered." The Sheriff displayed stained teeth as he smiled his best 'I got you' smile. He then patted French on his leg and left the room. The leg blossomed in pain. It seems the Doctor hadn't itemized all of French's injuries, or then, maybe he had.

It was obvious that the Doctor didn't care much for the Sheriff's bedside manner, and waited 'til he cleared the room to speak to his patient.

"You take it easy for a few days and I'll be back to check in on you. My daughter Helen will stay behind to change your bandages and keep track of your progress. She's a skilled physician in her own right, and this will be a good exercise for her."

The Doctor donned his coat and retrieved his hat, and then walked out to the kitchen to give final instruction to Zachariah's wife for the care and feeding of his patient.

Rue French had never dealt with a woman doctor before, but he saw this as an asset, and perhaps a means of influencing things in his favor, thereby aiding in his escape. But he had thought too soon.

"So, Helen is it? How is it a pretty girl like you decides to become a doctor of all things?" French didn't feel very handsome right then, but putting on the charm had never failed with the ladies before.

Helen didn't immediately answer French, but instead reached into her leather bag, and confidently pulled out a nasty looking .44 caliber pistol. She smiled as she aimed it right at French's head.

"It's easy. I like to shoot lying scoundrels like yourself, and then I patch them up so I can shoot them again. And by the way, thanks for bringing back my father's horse. It was stolen while Pa was up in Philadelphia last week. Seems you've been taking good care of it in the meantime." Helen then sat back and smiled, still holding the gun steady on her patient.

A murderer and a horse thief, too? French suddenly realized he could end up as hanging fodder with or without a name.

# CHAPTER FIVE

R ue French spent three long days and nights in bed before he was allowed to sit up. The knot on his head
had come to a peak, and Doctor Helen had expertly applied
leeches to relieve the pressure. But in his fevered state, and
with the drugs she had given him to ease the pain, French
had talked in his sleep, saying things he wouldn't want folks to
know--and Helen Williams was a very good listener.

That next morning the Sheriff and the Doctor once again
stood beside the bed, not even bothering to knock. They
watched as French held tightly to a chair and tried to plant
his feet firmly on the wood plank floor, a difficult task as the
room was busy spinning around him. He knew that he needed to get up and out of there if he was going to save his hide.
Always the fighter, he was not going to let a little light-headed
nausea keep him down any longer. He walked--one step, then
two, then three, and then he fell. Strong arms caught him on

the way down and lifted him back onto the bed. That would be enough walking for one day.

But this session was not over. Sheriff Hoskins sat himself down in that same chair, and bending over the bed, read the charges to be placed against French.

"Since we have not been able to find out your name as yet, I have taken the liberty of calling you 'Mr. Smith' with mentions of your condition included in the paperwork." He then unrolled the parchment and commenced reading.

"You, Mr. Smith, are hereby charged with the deaths of Amos Trotter and his wife Emma Trotter, whose bodies were found in the wreckage of their home some four days prior. Furthermore, you are charged with the wanton destruction of that same home in your attempt to cover up their deaths. In an unrelated matter, you are also hereby charged with horse thievery, specifically the known mount owned by Doctor Williams here. Mr. Smith, or whoever you are, how do you plead to these charges?"

This was surely the dangdest inquest French had ever been a part of. 'Mr. Smith' indeed. If they intended to hang him, he'd make the county pay for a trial first. The longer he played out his hand, weak as it was, the better chance he had to escape.

"I am not guilty, whatever my name is." This brought a chuckle from the Doctor, who had found the Sheriff's clumsy pomposity a great source of amusement. He had known the lawman for some years now, and had always marveled at the fellow's habit of using big words to hide small ideas. The Sheriff grunted his disapproval at the chuckling and then reluctantly pulled out a second document.

"Doctor Williams, having served this community as coroner for these many years, has determined that the Trotters had succumbed from the noxious gases seeping through the ground at their home site, and more than likely died in their sleep many weeks before your arrival at their farm. We have found in the rubble a lantern, recently used, most likely by yourself as you examined what must have seemed to be a vacant house, and as the explosion, which was witnessed by several neighbors, occurred early into the night, the charges of murder, and of destruction of property are hereby dropped, following common laws regarding the seeking of shelter in abandoned buildings."

"Whereas the horse in question had been returned within five miles of its owner's home, and that the horse had actually been stolen in Philadelphia, and out of this jurisdiction, and that the animal itself was none the worse for wear, the good Doctor has agreed not to press charges, and in turn thanks you for the return of said animal." The Sheriff had gone a long way to get there, but finally got to the point--no charges remained against him.

French just lay there, not totally believing what he had just heard. He wasn't going to hang after all, at least not today. Still, he realized, given his lifestyle and his past, a noose, a bullet, or a knife would likely mark the end of him sooner or later --- just not today.

The small crowd filed out of the room, leaving only Helen behind with her relieved patient. She once again checked him for fever and adjusted his covers.

"We'll try walking again tomorrow. No need to rush these things. Head wounds like this one can take some time to heal. You try to get some sleep now, and I'll check in on you later. Sleep tight John Cummins."

French cringed as panic swept through every inch of his body. Somehow, some way, she had learned his name!

John Cummins, aka Mr. Smith, didn't get much rest that day, or during the night either. She knew his name! What else did she know? He figured he must have somehow talked in his sleep, that's all it could be. He had to get out of there. He hadn't used his real name in years, and couldn't think of five people still living on this earth who knew him by that name. That had been very long ago.

The girl hadn't mentioned anything about talking in his sleep, and as far as he knew, he never had. But what with his head being eaten by leeches and who knows what drugs she had been feeding him, he could have said or done just about anything.

No matter. He knew he needed to make a run for it. His head still hurt, but his vision had cleared. His leg was badly bruised and his ankle stiff to walk on, but he had dealt with pain before. It was certain he wasn't going to outrun anyone. It appeared that he had been cleared of horse thievery just in time to go steal another one.

It wasn't like he wasn't grateful. The Doctor had been very kind to drop the charges, and Helen had done a pretty good job of patching him up, he would have to admit. But he wasn't likely to forget that she opened up their doctor-patient relationship by pointing a gun at his head. He chuckled to himself at that—he'd had that kind of effect on women before.

Morning was inching its way over the hills, and there was finally enough light in the room that French could see his way around. His hat was nowhere to be seen, but his trousers and boots were next to the chair over by the wall. He stood himself up and waited for the room to stop spinning. Leaning against the wall, French made his way over to the chair, and catching up his trousers, wisely sat down before he tried to get dressed. He had no knowledge of the layout of the house, or of the property surrounding the place either. But a few things usually rang true on farms like this. The outbuildings and stables were almost always downwind from the house, to keep those particular odors floating off in the other direction. In addition, the house would usually face the road, so a fellow could tell who was coming and going. Lastly, and in this case most importantly, the bedrooms were typically all in the same end of the house.

That meant that trying to sneak down the hallway would more than likely wake somebody up if they weren't up already. That would be a bad choice. The better choice would be the window. But French wasn't all that sure he could lift his leg up far enough to get through the opening without tipping over first. After all, it had been a Herculean effort just to put his pants on. And he had his boots yet to try. This wasn't going to be easy. French gritted his teeth, grabbed a boot, and commenced to pulling on the boot strap. Outside he could hear voices. There were men talking out in the yard, over to where he assumed was the front entrance. He recognized the voice of the Sheriff, but the other fellow he didn't know. He had no idea why the Sheriff would be coming back so soon, and this early in the day. But French was pretty well certain it wasn't a social call. He now had only one boot left to go.

Time was against him. The sun was coming up. He needed to get away---now! With a mighty pull the second boot was on. Stumbling and already exhausted from the effort, French lunged for the window, and throwing open the sash, dove head first out of the house and onto the ground below.

That hurt. That hurt a lot. He'd been hurting a lot lately. Using the wall for balance, he pulled himself up, working his way toward the barn, and hopefully toward a horse and freedom.

Using everything he could find to lean on, French steadied himself as he walked, the pain in his head and leg being overcome by his instinct for survival. So far, so good. He had not been discovered. But it would only be a matter of minutes now. He needed to stop and catch his breath, but he couldn't, there wasn't time. And then he was there, inside the barn. He had made it. Now to pick out a horse and get clear of this place.

But luck was not his this day, for Rue French saw two things he wasn't expecting to find in that barn that morning. For one thing, there were no horses in the barn at all, his escape plan foiled before it began. The other surprise was the vision of the lovely young Helen, half-dressed and holding a familiar looking pistol in her hand.

"I don't know what you're doing here, mister, but out this way when a man sees a girl in her underwear, it's the same as a proposal to marriage. Either that or you're up to no good. So, what'll it be? Do I send for the Preacher or the Sheriff?"

French just stood there, stupid like. There was very little of this young woman that was hidden from view, and even in the soft morning light, he could tell she was a beauty. Helen was enjoying the moment.

"Cat got your tongue, eh? Well, you might just as well come up closer and get a good look. Heaven knows I've seen plenty of you in the last week or so. We'll just call it even."

French wanted to run, but instead, like a moth to a flame, he actually took the lady's suggestion and limped boldly right on over to where she stood. Gently pushing the pistol downward, he took the girl in his arms and kissed her, and a proper kiss it was. There was no resistance, none whatsoever. She took a moment or two to recover from this man's unexpected advances. Then she smiled.

"Thank you, I think I needed that. And now, you scoundrel, turn yourself around and get back in bed. You've seen enough." With that, the pistol came back up as she threw a shirt over her shoulders with her other hand to cover herself. The show was over.

French bowed in the most gentlemanly way he knew how, and turning smartly, made his way back out the barn door and on toward the house. As a doctor, Helen Williams was skilled. But as a woman, she was clearly amazing—he was feeling much better already.

# CHAPTER SIX

R ue French was feeling pretty good about things right then. It had been awhile since he had kissed any girl, let alone one of her caliber. The fact that she had been half undressed and a beauty to boot didn't diminish the experience one bit.

He was so busy congratulating himself on his good fortune that he had plumb forgot about the voices he had heard from his bedroom just before he flung himself out the window on his so-far unsuccessful attempt to escape. His memory was quickly restored about five steps beyond the barn door as the Sheriff came out of the house accompanied by a man dressed in black with a face that was all business. French stopped in his tracks, not quite knowing what to do next. He stood there, unarmed, unprepared, and a long way from the bed where he was supposed to be resting. The Sheriff spoke first.

"Mr. Smith, er..uh..whoever you are, there's a fellow here come all the way from Philadelphia looking for you, or at least I think he's looking for you." As before, the Sheriff proved that he did not have a way with words.

"Matthew Tullen, sir." The big man in the dark clothing introduced himself and walked right up to French with his hand out. French took Tullen's hand and accepted the greeting. At least he wasn't being handcuffed—yet.

"I represent the Albany and Scranton Railroad, Mr. Smith. I have some property that may belong to you, that is if you are indeed the man I am looking for. The Sheriff here says you took a nasty blow to the head and have not yet recovered all of your memory. It's possible that the items I brought with me here today may help in some regard. Perhaps if you would be so kind as to step inside for a moment, we could get some things cleared up."

French was convinced that this man was some kind of law man or some such. Tullen was much too slick a character to be taken lightly. Unlike the local Sheriff here, this man knew his stuff and acted the part. French would need to tread lightly, as he had no hole card to play except for the false amnesia routine that Helen had seemed to have already sniffed out. This was a time to speak very little and listen very much.

They went on inside and sat at the table in the kitchen. French hadn't seen this room before, as he had been kept in that back bedroom since he'd arrived. He liked what he saw.

All in all, this little farm was quite pleasant. He had already noticed the many flowers planted around the house as he jumped out of the window, and now that he was inside, he came to appreciate the neat orderliness of the place. It wasn't all that different from the home he'd grown up in, and fond memories started to find their way back again. If only. . .

"Mr. Smith, we're looking for a man who went missing from a train just a few short miles from Philadelphia a week or so ago. The man in question meets your description to a 'T', and after conferring with the Sheriff here, I believe that with the similarities of the papers you had on your person, and those found in this luggage that I have in my possession, we have more than likely found our man." Then reaching behind his chair, Tullen produced a carpetbag, the very bag French had left behind on that train the night he and Bo Findley had fallen over the railing and into the ravine.

French's heart raced. The money! The weapons! The false identities! It was there for all to see, and he rightly assumed that it all had been viewed by Tullen before now.

"Mr. Smith, do you recognize this bag, or any of the items that are in the bag?" Tullen started to pull things out, one by one, as he spoke. His voice was calm and smooth, and had no threat to it at all. Already on the table lay French's shaving kit, a pistol with boxes of extra ammunition, a mirror, a leather wrap of small tools and knives, some clothes, and lastly, a very large bundle of money along with a heavy bag of coins.

Finally, Tullen produced a deck of business cards, printed for the likes of several different names and professions. These Tullen placed directly in front of French, a wry smile on his face, the final piece of the puzzle.

"If you would be so kind, Mr. Smith, please look through these business cards and tell us all just which one you are. Take your time, we're in no hurry here."

"There will be no need for that." The voice came from the doorway. The men, busy in their conversation had not noticed the girl slipping into the room.

"His name is Mr. John Cummins."

No one moved, no one spoke. French stared at Helen in disbelief. The woman who had so wonderfully filled his thoughts just a few minutes before had now given away his deepest secret. He didn't trust women, and now that sentiment burned deeper than ever. His leg started hurting again.

"Well then, Mr. uh Cummins, it seems as though you are quite the hero." Tullen went into what seemed to be a reasonably prepared speech, as though he was anxious to get this over and done with.

"You see, sir, I represent the Albany and Scranton Railroad in matters of property and protection. Most folks would call me a railroad detective."

French sat and listened, trying hard not to look back at Helen, or say anything at all. Something didn't make sense here, and until he knew what it was, he'd just stay quiet. After all, how is a man going to be able to talk himself out of something, if he doesn't yet know what it is he's gotten himself into to talk himself out of?

"It seems that a man fitting your description took it upon himself to confront a would-be highwayman who had drawn a weapon and was apparently intending to rob the passengers on that train. Witnesses claim that you single handedly, and unarmed, wrestled with that man in an attempt to subdue him, and that your fight took the two of you to the end of the passenger car and off into a ravine not far from the Philadelphia terminal. A subsequent search of the area found no trace of either you or of the assailant. It was a 'missing persons' bulletin with your description filed by the Sheriff here that led me to you."

French glanced over to the Sheriff, and then up to Helen. She was looking at him now with admiration and respect. The

Sheriff seemed annoyed at best. Neither of them had any real idea as to the truth of the matter, and he saw no sane reason to dispute Tullen's story. The Detective went on.

"So moved by your heroics were these folks, that they acted quickly to secure your bag and coat in hopes that they might be returned to you somehow, along with their heartfelt gratitude. The directors of the railroad have made it my personal duty to track you down and return your property, along with this voucher for one thousand dollars which you can cash at any bank."

This was all crazy talk. Hero? Reward money? It was all French could do to keep from laughing out loud.

"Mr. Cummins, all I need you to do is sign this paper showing that I have completed my task, and then the money, the bag, and its contents are yours once again." The Detective produced a sealed ink pen from his pocket, and handed it to French along with this very official looking document.

Under any other set of circumstances, French would have read every word with great scrutiny and care before touching the pen. After all, it could all be a trick to get him to sign a carefully worded admission of guilt to any number of sins of commission he had been involved with in these last many years. But in this case, seeing how he was now the hero type, to do so would be to doubt the sincerity of the people there around him. He signed the paper in his real name, with one little exception. He purposely spelled Cummins with only one "m".

This formality complete, the men stood to shake hands to seal the deal. But it wasn't to be.

At that very instant the room was blown to pieces in a deadly hail of gunfire. Rue French's enemies had found him.

# CHAPTER SEVEN

The window glass exploded into the room, showering its occupants with a deadly barrage of shrapnel. Those glass shards were accompanied by a scattering of wooden splinters equally as lethal as the bullets which had created them. Zachariah had been leaning against the table, listening to the conversation while nursing a cup of Irish coffee, his typical morning wake-me-up. A bullet caught his arm, and spun him around. He caught his chin on the edge of the cast iron cook stove as he fell, and was out cold before he hit the floor.

French had just started to rise from his chair but the soreness in his leg caused him to hesitate on the way up. That sore leg saved his life, as the bullet that glanced off his shoulder would have more than likely pierced his heart, given the chance.

The Sheriff and the Detective weren't hit in the barrage, and immediately returned fire with their pistols, but with no idea who they were shooting back at through the ruined window.

Helen had let out a startled scream when the glass shattered, but quickly moved over to the fallen men, first to Zachariah, then to French. There wasn't much she needed to do for Zach, who was out cold but had a good strong pulse. French had already stuffed a kerchief under his shirt and seemed to be alright for now. She gave him a quick kiss on the cheek, and then hurried to the back bedroom to retrieve her bag. A voice called out from the woods beyond.

"Rue French! We know you're in there! Come out and we'll get this done and over with. No need for these innocent folks to get hurt. We'll give you one minute or we open up again!"

The two lawmen looked at each other in puzzled amazement. Rue French, here? French was a known killer and thief, and reputed for being as bad a man as anyone cared to deal with. But Helen said the stranger's name was Cummins. There must be some mistake.

"Hold on a minute!" The Detective was a man of action and hoped to get their assailants talking, if for no other reason than to spot out their positions.

"There's no one here by the name of French. You've got no reason to be shooting this place up. And you've already injured some innocent people!"

"Minute's up!" Once again the room lit up with gunfire. The Sheriff caught one in the leg and the spices on the stove turned to dust. Helen was back with her bag in one hand and Zachariah's rifle in the other.

"I'm going to the side window. Next time they open up, I'll see if I can pick one off." Before the Detective could say anything, the girl was gone, rifle in hand. He had to admit, the girl had spunk.

41

Helen settled herself under the window sill in the next room. Luckily the weather was still warm so the window was already part way open. There was no risk in drawing attention to her position by opening the sash. She then reached into her bag and pulled out a pair of darkened glasses, the kind used to treat folks with eyes too sensitive to see in bright sunlight. She hoisted out the rifle, judged the distance to where she figured the shooters were hidden, and waited. She wouldn't have to wait for long.

It seems that some folks just aren't all that bright. And folks who steal and rob for a living are often among the dumbest of all. Any ten year old Indian boy knows the need to continue to change your position during a fight to make it harder for your enemy to turn you into a target. The men who were shooting up the house from the woods beyond were not equal to ten year old Indians.

Helen set herself up on the sill of the side window and waited for the next volley to come. With the morning light behind them, the muzzle flashes had proved impossible to get a fix on. But she figured that wearing those heavily darkened glasses would give her an edge. She might have had the Sheriff or the Detective use them, but there was no time for schooling here, and as she was very familiar with those glasses, and their use, the task was hers to complete.

Zach's rifle was a single shot cartridge model, and she had over a dozen shells to work with. She had no idea who had made the weapon or what model it was and couldn't care less. All she asked was that it shot straight and true. The rest would be up to her. She steadied herself and waited.

Sure enough, they fired again. Helen figured they might be using single shot rifles themselves, as they always fired in volleys. If she could load faster, it could work to her advantage.

The glasses worked! She could clearly see the muzzle flashes, three of them. She aimed the barrel where the middle flash had come from, and then moved her aim to the right at what she figured to be about three feet and then down a foot. Then she let them have it.

Immediately she heard a terrible scream and then shouts. She knew she'd hit something, so she quickly reloaded, sighted a foot to the left and fired again, guessing that whoever had been to the fellow's right would have moved to come to the aid of his fallen partner.

The shooting stopped. French was up and moving about, pistol in hand. He crossed over to the window where Helen had been firing. What he saw there was a lovely woman holding a deadly looking rifle out a window frame, and wearing the strangest looking spectacles he'd ever seen. But there was another, more ominous detail--a dark stream of blood running down her back from her shoulder to her waist. If it hurt, and it had to, she wasn't saying anything about it.

"You're hurt." French moved toward her, careful not to show himself through the window.

"I know. But so are they. They tried to kill us, John, all of us, and I think they would have, given the chance. I think I got one, maybe two, or they could just as well be playing possum hoping to draw us out in the open. I'll be alright for now. How are the others?"

French was more than impressed by the guts and fortitude this young lady had shown. Earlier he had been delighted by her form, now he was taken in by her substance. He'd known a lot of girls in his day, mostly of the dance hall variety, but he had never known a woman like this. It caused him to reconsider what he knew about women.

"Zachariah is moaning so I know he's alive. I put a towel under his head to make him more comfortable. The Sheriff caught one in the leg and quickly tied his scarf around it and kept on firing. The Detective seems to be alright. Have you seen anything of Zach's wife and boy?"

"They headed out for town with the wagon before first light. I woke up when Gabe came into the barn to fetch the horses. That's why I got up to get dressed. The boy spends a lot of his time looking through the cracks in the barn wood trying to get a glimpse of me while I change. I figured with him gone, it would be safe. Then you walked in." She spoke quietly, but never took her eye off the trees.

"Sorry, I didn't know you were in there. I came in looking for a horse. I thought I'd take a ride."

"Well, I certainly hope you weren't too awfully disappointed to find me instead of a horse. Still, I'm not the least bit sorry. The look on your face was worth every bit of my lost modesty. I'd do it again if I thought I'd get the same reaction. The kiss, however, was something I hadn't expected. Thank you. It had been awhile since the last one."

Now why would this woman be thanking him for looking at her half-dressed and then kissing her without so much as a 'by your leave'? But then French had given up trying to figure out womenfolk long ago. It was a thing best left alone.

Several minutes had passed by now, and no more shots had come from the edge of the woods. Then they heard a horse riding away, and in a hurry to be gone. After a few more minutes' wait, French figured he'd waited enough. Always a man on the attack, French once again climbed out his bedroom window, this time a little more gracefully, and circled around the corrals and behind the barn. He was able to work his way through the brush and came up behind two tied off horses.

Helen said she had seen three flashes, and as they had heard one horse ride off, the math made sense. It was only a short few steps to where two bodies lay.

One man was obviously dead, the front of his face blown away. The second man lay dazed and dying, a wound in his chest just left of his heart. He looked up at French and weakly lifted his hand as a sign of surrender.

"No more, French. Let me go like this. No more, please." Then he coughed up blood. It was only a matter of minutes now.

French recognized the man, but didn't know his name. He reached over and pushed the man's rifle aside and knelt close by, his weapon still drawn.

"Who sent you after me? Why are you all trying to kill me? Who gave the order?" French heard his voice getting louder, and understood that the stress was getting to him. He had to get a grip and fast.

"My name is Chet Gillen. Please have someone put my name on the marker. There's money in my saddlebags to pay for it. And write to my Ma in Pittsburgh, Bessie Gillen. Tell her I was a good man. Tell her I died in an accident. Send her what's left of the money. It's all I have. Pa died in the war. I was going to get ten thousand for killing you, French. Then I could have gone home a rich man and gotten her out of that dirty place. Now she'll have nothing. I made a bad bargain."

"I'll do it, just as you ask. I promise. Tell me, Gillen, while you can, who sent you and why?" French needed an answer fast as this man was nearly gone.

"You know why. And now he wants you dead. You should have never done it. No girl is worth what all you're going to suffer. Remember my Ma, you promised." Chet then closed his eyes, and took a deep breath, his last. French leaned back and watched as life slipped away from the man who lay before him. How many men had he watched die? What kind of man had he become to have seen so many--caused so many?

"Did you know him?" Somehow French had failed to notice that the Detective had come up behind him. Tullen stood over him, pistol in hand.

"How much did you hear?" French didn't want to kill this man, too, but he was already in too deep to stop now.

"Enough to know that you're worth ten thousand dead." The Detective slowly holstered his gun and looked French square in the eye. "You've lived this life for too long, my friend. Something tells me that John Cummins died years ago, and that you have taken his place, in spirit if not in body. I could have shot you and collected the prize for myself and you know it. Fact is, I figured you for a highwayman from the beginning. But I get paid to return things to their rightful owners, and to protect the property of the Albany and Scranton Railroad. As long as you don't bother us, we won't bother you." He turned and started walking back to the house. Then he stopped.

"By the way, Mister Cummins, the girl in there asked me to tell you to get back inside right away. Something about you doctoring her up. Seems she's been hit."

French had completely forgotten about Helen and the wound on her back. He was too worried about himself. Bad leg or no, French somehow beat the Detective to the door, but then turned and gave the man an order.

"Ride back into town and fetch the Doctor, and Zach's wife and boy as well. We need help out here."

The Detective nodded in agreement, and finding his horse, took off at a gallop. French didn't bother to watch him go. Tullen was too good a man to need watching. He hurried inside.

The Sheriff had slid over to give aid to Zachariah, who still didn't seem aware of his surroundings. He gave French the high sign that he was alright, and pointed to the next room where Helen had set up her defense.

French found her there, on the floor in a pool of blood, eyes closed, and not moving. French gently picked her up, and with his leg no longer mattering, carried her limp form to the bed he had so recently called home. He laid her face down, carefully turning her head so that she could breathe easier. Taking out his clasp knife, he cut open her shirt.

He would need to work quickly.

# CHAPTER EIGHT

F rench hated having to cut open Helen's blouse like that, what with such beautiful embroidery on the neck and sleeves and all. But if he didn't stem the flow of blood, and soon, they might very well have to bury her in it. He couldn't allow that. Besides, he figured, as blood stained as it was, she would never bother to wear it again anyway.

Her skin was soft to the touch as he wiped away the blood with the same towel that lay nearby. He could feel his shoulder still seeping but didn't care. He'd bled before this, and more than once.

French was surprised, however, when he got down to her wound. She hadn't been shot as he had assumed, but rather she had a large shard of glass protruding just under her shoulder blade. It must have pierced her back when the window glass shattered during the first volley. The pain had to have been intense and spoke volumes of this young woman who was able to think clearly through it all and somehow dream up a scheme to defeat their attackers, while all the men in the building did was spray a lot of lead around. In fact, French was ashamed that he hadn't even gotten off a decent shot.

It took three tries before French was able to get enough grip on the slippery shard to pull it out. The glass had gone in much deeper than he had expected, which explained why she was bleeding so much. He was surprised to see that the bleeding somehow slowed after the glass had been pulled free. He wasn't expecting that.

Rue French was no doctor, although he had posed as one on more than one occasion to swindle a dollar or two. But now, suddenly, he was pressed into life and death service with what little medical knowledge he had. Any kid growing up on the frontier in his day knew the basics of first aid, and could even set a bone or work a splint if need be. And it wasn't like he hadn't bound the wound of an unlucky compatriot from time to time. But it might be hours before her father and the others would be able to reach the farm. The Sheriff was holding his own but unable to move around much, and Zach was still woozy at best.

It was up to him to save his girl. His girl? What was he thinking? He had no room in his life for a woman. But try as he did, he couldn't shake the thought. So then, it was true. French realized that he was starting to fall in love with Helen Williams, and that he could not lie his way out of it, not even to himself. There was still too much blood. The wound had to be closed, but he didn't have rolls of cloth needed to do the job. He could hold the skin together and stop the flow, but he knew that sooner or later his hands would lose their grip, causing the wound to pull open again. And then he got an idea, a crazy idea at best, but better than any other option he could think of.

He got up slowly, which was all his swollen leg would allow, and bolted out the front door in a hurry, back out to where the two men still lay dead and unattended to. French had no time for them. Just beyond that place stood a grove of sweet smelling pine trees, big and strong. This is what he needed.

Using his clasp knife once again, he gathered globs of fresh pine sap, wiping them onto the towel. When he figured he had enough, he rushed back into the house, ignoring the questions the Sheriff was bothering him with. There would be time for talk later.

On the way through the kitchen, he located a clean towel, and sitting once again on the bed beside her, he carefully wiped and cleaned blood from the wound. He then used his fingers to apply the sticky sap to each side of the cut, and tearing off a clean piece of cloth from her blouse, carefully pulled the two sides together as tight as he could, gluing the cloth down into the sap to hold the skin closed in place. It had always been hard for him to get sap off his fingers and clothes in the past, and he hoped it would work here to hold the wound together as well.

French finished up by covering Helen's back with the rest of the clean cloth, and then a blanket. At that moment he felt so inadequate, so inept in his efforts, and yet he'd done all he could do. He brought the chair over and sat down beside her, holding her hand in his. He brushed her hair away from her face, lovingly, anxiously, and looked down upon her, wishing he could have done more. All this was his fault. Those men had come for him, for who he was, and for who he had become. And then he whispered words that came from his troubled soul, "I love you, Helen Williams." And so, he had said it, right out loud, and he felt better for the saying of it.

Then the girl surprised him again, and more than likely not for the last time. She had been awake the whole time.

"I love you, too, John Cummins. You did fine." And she smiled, and fell into a deep sleep.

It was well past noon by the time the Doctor arrived at the house, with Tullen riding alongside. About ten minutes later, a whole slew of folks showed up in wagons and on horseback to aid in what the gossips were already calling a massacre.

Doc Williams was a true professional, and coming through the door, stopped to check on the Sheriff and Zach first. Soon strong arms were there to help carry these men off to the two remaining beds where they could be cleaned up and prepared for the Doctor's attentions.

He then walked into the room where French had been a patient for all those days, being watched over by his daughter. Now the tables had turned, with the man she had been nursing, now keeping watch over her. The Doctor could not hide the agony and fear that swept over him, seeing his only child lying face down on the bed, with blood-stained towels laying nearby. Williams noted the blood running down the back of French's shoulder, now clotted and stiff, and how he was holding his little girl's hand, somehow willing her to get well.

"I need you to let me have that chair for a minute son, so I can check her over." The Doctor was trying to stay calm, even though he could see the amount of carnage that had been done here. First he took her hand and found her pulse--strong and steady, and he let out a puff of air in relief. Next he slowly pulled back the blanket to examine what he figured to be the wound. Then he simply sat and stared.

"Tell me everything you have done here young man."

And so French slowly and carefully told his story, step by step, with probably far more detail than the Doctor needed to hear. When he got to the part about the tree sap and the cloth, the Doctor was nearly speechless.

"Where did you come up with that idea?" The Doctor was amazed and a little amused as well. He was curious to know just how the man he still knew only as 'Mr. Smith' would come up with an idea like that.

"I don't know. It just came to me. I was desperate to close up the wound and stop the bleeding. I'm sorry, I didn't know what to do." Despair and worry showed on French's face. The Doctor now saw a side of this man he had never seen before.

"Well, it just so happens that the Indians around these parts have been using sticky sap for things like this since long before the white man ever came to these shores. I'm pleased to see that you kept from getting any in the wound itself, as that could have caused some trouble." Then he surprised French in a way that he would never forget.

"So, Helen, how do you feel?" He looked up at French then with a knowing, cat-like grin that beat the band.

"I think I'm gonna be just fine, Pa, but it may take a day or two. By the way, I'd like introduce you to Mister John Cummins. He and I are going to be married."

French just stood there with his mouth hung open and nothing to say. Why that little fraud, playing possum like that! Married? Well, she had told him back in the barn, either the Sheriff or the Preacher, hadn't she?

# CHAPTER NINE

I t was two weeks to the day from when French had been brought to the Shartle farm, that he was well enough to resume his ride south. He felt strong again, and was anxious to meet up with McPhearson and somehow straighten this mess out. Already five men were dead, and with such a price on his head, that number was surely to grow--with the strong possibility of his number being one of them.

A lot had happened since the attack, and things would never be the same there again. The railroad Detective had stayed around for a few days to help the Sheriff get things in order and for the dead assailants to be buried. Some of the money found in those men's pockets went toward their burial, complete with markers, but most of the rest went toward the repair of Mrs. Shartle's kitchen, which had taken the brunt of the attack. French kept his promise, and sent a letter along with the thousand dollars the railroad had awarded him, to

Bessie Gillen in Pittsburgh. The railroad Detective agreed to see to it that the letter was delivered safely into her hands. In the letter, French said that Chet had died a hero, fighting off a notorious bandit. At least it wasn't a total lie.

Mrs. Shartle had been magnificent. Upon returning home in haste, she found her husband still knocked senseless, the Sheriff pooling blood across her wood plank floor, her windows and door frame in shambles, and the Doctor's daughter, Helen, lying face down on the bed which she had so recently set aside for the care of a stranger known only to her as 'Mr. Smith.'

But with her son's help, things were soon put right, and a warm delicious stew was in the pot, ready to feed the many who had come to help. The Sheriff was hauled back to town on a wagon, where the Doctor would finish tending to his wounds.

Zachariah had always suffered from a glass jaw, and his wife was grateful for him hitting his chin on the edge of the stove, as it probably saved his life, seeing how he was on the floor when most of the bullets came flying. The injury to his arm was small enough that it would heal quickly. Meanwhile his son was happy to pick up the slack while his father healed up. Gabe was a son to be proud of.

The Doctor had stitched up the small crease in French's shoulder in no time at all, and then finished up his daughter's back wound, still praising French for his quick work in closing up the gash using the pine sap.

"The Indians have been using pine sap for things like this for years. Those fellows knew more about the plants and flowers around us than we'll ever know. It's a shame really. If the white man had spent more time learning from the Indians instead of shooting them, we'd all be better off." The Doctor, while seldom known to be talkative, tended to go on and on when something as important as stitching needed to be done. Peace and quiet had returned to the Shartle farm as night fell, neighbors and friends having long since returned home. Needed repairs had already begun.

Helen quickly improved as the days passed. Still, it seemed that the loss of blood, coupled with the ferocity of the attack, had taken something out of her. She was weak, and spent most of her time sitting on the porch reading. It hurt to move her arm. Helen had not again mentioned the idea of the marriage that she had so boldly announced to her father only a few days before. She now spoke to John Cummins only when spoken to. Noticing the change, the Doctor took John aside, and walking out toward the barn, said as much as he thought he should.

"Mr. Cummins, there are some things you need to know about my daughter, and I guess I'm the one to tell you. She told me about your walking into the barn and finding her half-dressed, and of what transpired afterward. If you were the cad most folks think you are, or should I say, the cad you want most folks to think you are, you would have forced yourself upon her right then and there. But you didn't, and somehow I know you wouldn't. Still, I thank you."

"The truth is, about three years ago a man came into her life and completely swept Helen off her feet. He had money and the kind of strong good looks that girls seem to fall for. She was already a full grown woman, beautiful like her mother, God rest her soul, and that man took notice, and took advantage. When all was said and done, he had taken her innocence and her pride, and left her carrying a child who was stillborn six months later. Since then I've kept her busy learning doctoring and such, and she seems to have a great knack for such things. I had hoped to send her off for further schooling last spring but she wouldn't go. I'm afraid the hurt still runs very deep in her, and it breaks my heart to see it."

"And then you come along and mess everything up. In some ways you resemble that other fellow, and when she saw you all banged up like that, she insisted on staying on and caring for you. Maybe I'm a fool, but I gave in and let her have her way. She knew what you were from the start, and I guess this was her way of getting through the memory."

"At least that's what I thought, until I walk in and see that you've probably saved her life with your pine sap trick, and then she goes and tells me she intends to marry you---something about a Preacher or a Sheriff."

French just stood there. He wanted to say something, but he couldn't. Her words of marriage had flattered him, she being so pretty and wise and all. And now he comes to find out that she was more than likely using him to help rid her of the bad memory of a man who hurt her badly and then left her high and dry. The parallels of the troubles in his life and the troubles in hers were vivid in his mind. He understood her pain far better than he would want others to know. A new plan began to form in his mind--a way to even the score with this lout, and maybe help her to move on as well.

And in those few moments something reawakened in French's soul, like a door opening back to where John Cummins still dwelt as he had before, a man who had been gallant and trustworthy, a man of honor and truth. He now had a reason to be truly himself once again if only for the moment at hand.

"Tell me, what was that man's name?" The look in French's eye told the Doctor everything he needed to know. He knew at once what the man standing before him intended to do. And in this case, at this moment, a Doctor's oath was overcome by a father's rage. He told French what he wanted to know.

"His name was Jacob McPhearson."

# CHAPTER TEN

A nd so it was those two weeks later that John Cummins, aka Rue French, gathered himself up and rode away from the Shartle farm, with a heavy heart and a new-found purpose in life --- to find and kill Jacob McPhearson. But first he placed a sign at the front gate, written in hopes of protecting his hosts from any more mischief. It read:

I have gone to see McPhearson. Follow me there if you want.

Leave these people alone.        Rue French


The anger in French's heart was probably as much for himself as it was for Jacob. He had become what he was, or rather mostly what he wanted folks to think he was, mainly for the power it gave him over others, and the freedom to do as he pleased. No one beards the lion.

And yet, here he was, riding south through unknown territory, the target of every would-be thug on the eastern seaboard, and a captive to hidden places and dark corners. Even his parting words to Helen were now beginning to haunt him.

"I've got a job to do, and if it all goes well it'll make things better for both me and you. I have a score to settle, something hanging over my head like a noose. Maybe when it's all over I'll come back this way and look you up. I'm sure we have some things we need to talk over, but now's not the time. Get well young lady." Then he kissed her softly, and hurriedly walked out to his waiting horse, a horse that had formerly been ridden by one of the men who had come to kill him just days before.

All in all that had been about as lame a goodbye as any man had ever handed any good looking woman anywhere, anytime. But the truth of the matter was that following those few days where her life seemed to hang in the balance, French's feelings of love for this pretty blond girl seemed to wane into only a casual interest. It was a lot like wearing the same shirt day after day without a good washing in between. Things get sticky and uncomfortable, with no eager anticipation for the next time you have to put it on. That torch had gone out, and quickly enough. But Helen did hold a special place in French's heart --- he now had another reason to go gunning for Jacob McPhearson. It wasn't just about him anymore.

No one stood on the porch as he rode off that morning. No one had waved goodbye to Rue French. Things were once again just as they had been before. Wherever Rue French went, he always left a trail of dead bodies behind him. And now he was heading due south, the tally not yet complete.

Back in town, Matthew Tullen, the Albany and Scranton Railroad detective, was sharing a pot of coffee in Sheriff Hoskin's office, as the two compared notes while writing their reports concerning the recent events out at the Shartle farm. The reports would differ somewhat in content and perspective, but the facts and circumstances would pretty much read the same. The Sheriff had his swollen leg up on a chair, relying on whiskey to help stem the pain. The coffee cup was there for show.

"Do you think that fellow was really Rue French, the killer? I can't imagine a man with his reputation getting himself blown up in a building that way. I'd figure he'd be smarter than that." They had been discussing the man that the Doctor's daughter had declared to be John Cummins, and couldn't quite put the pieces together. The Detective had a different approach.

"Well, Sheriff, all I know for sure is that those three men who ambushed us were convinced that he was Rue French, and in their court of law, the rifles do the testifying. When it was over, I watched Cummins go out to where they lay. I followed close behind. That Gillen fellow was still alive, and I overheard the two of them talking. Come to find out, this man Rue French is worth $10,000 dead----period. And it seemed these two had known each other some time back. I can only figure it to be a blood feud of some sort. There are a few rewards out for this man French elsewhere, but no more than $500 or so, and all those for larceny and petty theft and such. $10,000 is a lot of money to put on a man's head. It must be for something pretty serious." The Sheriff had been looking off to nowhere as he listened to the Detective talk. It was a hard thing to reconcile, with what little he was paid to risk his life for the community day in and day out. The Sheriff shared his feelings.

"It just doesn't make sense. How is it that the slime and vermin of this world are worth thousands, while the true heroes, the lawmen, the teachers, even the army are paid so little? It's all upside down. Our society has its values in all the wrong places." The Sheriff poured himself another drink.

"I can't argue the point, Sheriff. Seems the people who do the most good are paid the least money. But of course, in this case, if one of those teachers picks up a gun and shoots this Rue French fellow, they will suddenly be worth $10,000 themselves. I guess it's a matter of doing bad to make good. But then, all those two fellows we found laying there in that ditch back at Shartle's farm will get for their trouble is six feet of dirt. Pennsylvania has fine dirt mind you, but it's not worth $10,000."

The Sheriff only heard a portion of what the Detective had said just then. He was too busy feeling sorry for himself, sitting there in that dingy office with his leg all wrapped up. A dollar a day plus keep. It just wasn't right.

An hour or so later the Detective left, with the promise to stay in touch, a promise he had no intention of keeping. For his part, the Sheriff never did like men who dressed as well as Tullen, mostly because he knew he couldn't afford to measure up. He was glad to see him go.

He'd been Sheriff there in that town for about ten years now, and enjoyed an adequate but simple living. He wasn't married, never had been, and generally felt uncomfortable around women folks. Too sneaky for his taste.

He hadn't always been a lawman, in fact, he'd spent more than a few years dodging the very laws he was now upholding, as a gang member up in New York City. It was a rough and tumble life, and he'd been pretty good with a knife in those days. Things got too hot, though, and he headed west to work on the canals and such. Running from his past, he set himself up as a candidate for Sheriff in the local election, and when his opponent ran off with a bar room girl, he was declared the winner by default. He had held the job ever since. A badge can be an excellent shield to hide behind if you're careful. He was very careful.

But it was hard to be careful with $10,000 right out there just out of reach. That Rue French fellow was a pretty sharp dresser himself as he remembered. And he had him right there dead to rights out at the Shartle farm all that time! If only he could prove who the man was...

Hoskins grimaced from the pain that shot up his leg as he moved to try to get more comfortable. He poured himself another drink. It just wasn't fair.

# CHAPTER ELEVEN

S tronton had worked quickly to transform the ancestral home of the O'Dells to a semblance of its former glory. It had been easy enough to find willing and capable hands to help with the rebuilding, what with scores of men looking for work after the war, their own homes destroyed and livelihoods lost.

Money gleaned from the ill-begotten gains of a crooked judge, the spoils from that man's illicit running of slaves and opium, was now being put to better use---the rebuilding of a world ravaged by war. But paint and nails couldn't heal all of the scars the war had left behind.

Stronton's daughter, Ginny, had become somber and quiet as of late. Those scars she carried didn't readily show, as she was always cordial and bright, and shared a willing smile whenever spoken to. But Stronton knew his daughter as he knew himself, and the deeply dug pit of shame and disgrace that the girl had endured would not be so easily filled with new memories and happy surroundings. She had grown to a beautiful young woman now, but had never had the chance to be called upon by a young man of good standing on a warm summer day. Her young womanhood had been one of torment, degradation, and shame.

He blamed himself. He should have been there. He was too busy off fighting a war that had long since been lost. His dear wife had been dead and buried long before he ever knew. He should have been there beside her during her last days, holding her hand, and telling of his love for her. And then it was only weeks later that Ginny was taken. Had he been there it would have never happened. He could have protected her. He felt like a fool.

Stronton enjoyed watching Ginny work tirelessly to move flowers and shrubs into position around the house. A new wing had been added, and the work was very nearly complete.

The General leaned casually against a column on the big wooden porch, now gleaming with its fresh coat of white paint. A chuckle greeted the girl as she made her way back inside to get dinner ready. She had dirt on her hands and dirt on her face, and dirt on her clothes, but he gave her a fatherly hug anyway. A little dirt must never be a barrier to affection.

Ginny smiled her smile, and giggled at her appearance, and then chided him for getting dirt on his clothes by hugging her. She went on inside to clean up.

Stronton watched her go, with a tear in his eye, thankful to God Almighty that he had been granted the privilege of sharing this moment with the daughter he had nearly lost forever. It was the most beautiful dirt he'd ever worn.

But as he turned to walk over to inspect his daughter's handiwork, a chill suddenly ran through his spine, with the memory of that day, not long ago, that he had impersonated a killer named Rue French in order to set his daughter free. He suddenly felt a tremor of dread, remembering that there was always a price to be paid for pulling the devil's chain.

A man such as Rue French would not tolerate the use of his name, not for any purpose, without collecting a fee for the privilege. A fee of great price.

French hadn't ridden two miles south from the Shartle farm when he came upon a horse and rider sitting motionless on the trail ahead of him. Whoever it might be, French did not know, but the fellow was there, waiting for him with rifle in hand, and the barrel was pointing his way.

French knew that this man was more than likely not alone. The word 'ambush' came to mind. But seeing how the man was just sitting and not shooting, French figured that he intended to do some talking first, and that some others were hidden nearby, waiting for a signal to fire the first shots.

There really wasn't anyone French wanted to talk to right at that moment. His goal was to get to Virginia where he figured to put this sort of nonsense to rest. It was unfortunate for the fellow blocking the road that he stood between Rue French and where he wanted to go—very unfortunate.

French's horse was fresh, and showed every indication that it would like to run off a little of the rust it had accumulated while spending time at the Shartle farm, waiting for him to get well enough to leave that place. While the horse had originally been ridden by one of French's would-be killers a week or so back, the actual lineage of ownership was most likely a matter for debate. But that man no longer had need of the horse, and French had taken a liking to the big gelding— a partnership of circumstance.

In one fluid and well-practiced motion, French put heels to his mount, let out a yell, and pulling his pistol, ran straight for the man blocking the road. The surprise couldn't have been more complete or the outcome more certain.

The would-be assailant was caught totally off guard, and tried to land a hurried and off balance shot at the charging French, only to be knocked from his saddle by French's return fire. French thought he heard shouts and hooves behind him as he ran past, and knew he had been right about the ambush. He had escaped, free and clear.

But a few moments later French did the unthinkable. He reined in, and spinning the horse around, charged full long toward the two riders who were pursuing him. The surprise move was devastating, and within a matter of seconds, two more saddles were emptied.

Three more men, dead. French turned once again and slowly walked his horse through the debris of battle, assessing the damage done, and looking for a survivor whom he could question, but there was none. Once again his boldness and skill had won the day, and once again men lay dead in his wake.

French knew he had been lucky this time, and the time before, and the time before that. He wondered to himself just how many others were already out on the road with visions of bounty money in their heads. Greed and the promise of easy money had caused many a man to do foolish things for which they were poorly prepared. Far too often in such matters the price of failure was death.

French didn't bother to collect the horses or to bury the dead. He just didn't care anymore. He thought about getting off the road and trying a less obvious route to Virginia, any sane man would. But he figured it just didn't matter. Time was his biggest enemy now. He needed to find McPhearson and get this thing settled once and for all. The quickest way to Virginia was this road.

He nudged his mount into a good trot, and started whistling a tune he knew when he was a boy. "Come and get me," he said to no one in particular. And he smiled, and scampered on.


Hours run into days on the open trail. Miles of loneliness and worry mix in together for a man on the run. The food was bad and the overnight lodging fell short in accommodations. French was worn out and hungry, and he needed to pull a swindle off somewhere to set things right for himself, and maybe lay low for a while. But not for long. Not with McPhearson's thugs out there gunning for him. Soon, very soon.

There was no sign along the road to tell French just when it was that he had ridden into Virginia, just as he possessed no road map that would let him know how to get to the farm where Jacob had taken up residency. He did know that the farm had been in the possession of a family named O'Dell for many generations, and that Jacob had lived there for a time as an orphan taken in by the O'Dell family. The rest all seemed kind of vague, excepting for that he had moved in uninvited, and took over the place when his dead brother's wife had taken ill and died.

Given that there had just been a war up and down the countryside, French figured that stories of lands and houses changing hands must be commonplace nowadays. It stood to reason that unscrupulous men could build a fortune taking advantage of folks during these uncertain times. Men such as himself, he reflected with only a small sense of regret. It was an opportunity he would look in to.

As there were now men out there trying to kill him for a bounty, he would need to be mighty careful about whom he spoke to or asked directions from. He needed a disguise that would belay all suspicion. He was still contemplating that problem when he rode past what looked to be an abandoned church. He smiled to himself. It just didn't get any easier than this.

# CHAPTER TWELVE

French had used this trick before, that of the traveling Preacher. He'd always been something of a silver-tongued devil, and could quote a verse or two when called upon. Whatever sense of conscience he had felt back there with Helen had quickly been extinguished by the events out there on the road. John Cummins' brief resurrection had now been replaced by the reality of Rue French, killer, thief, and once again, impostor.

The abandoned church meant that the folks around these parts were most likely in need of a shepherd, and with a little luck and a few contributions---along with a square meal or two, French figured to ride on, above suspicion from anyone who came around asking questions of his whereabouts. He planned to be long gone before Sunday services would commence.

A short ways from the old church stood a modest little cabin, built long ago by skilled hands, and nestled nicely in a grove of fruit trees. The place was in need of paint, but other than that seemed in good repair. A small shed of a barn stood nearby, about big enough to hold a horse or two and a buggy, but not much else.

French knew at once that this was no farmer's home, not with a barn so small, and figured rather that it might be the home of a doctor or such. It looked much too nice for a Preacher's home, especially with the church being in such disrepair.

There was only about an hour of sunlight left in the day, and it stood to reason that he should find a place to stay the night. This place looked to be just the ticket. French tied off the horse, and straightening his coat, walked confidently up to the door. There was a bell next to the door frame, with a heavy cord for pulling. He rang once, then twice, and prepared his best smile as the door opened.

She was old, with her hair up in a bun, wearing an apron over a print cotton dress. French couldn't guess her age, and wondered at who all might be living there with her. She seemed spry enough, and surprised him as she spoke.

"I know who you are, and I know why you're here, so you might just as well go put your horse up for the night and come in and set for supper. I've already made your bed up in back, and I'll be putting food on the table as soon as the biscuits come out of the oven. Hurry now, it'll be getting dark soon." She then closed the door and went back to her kitchen, leaving French standing before the door frame outside, wondering for the life of himself just what he had gotten himself into here. Still, he had been offered a bed for the night, and a hot meal was being served. All in all, things were coming along much better than expected.

He walked the horse to the shed and removed the saddle, spending a few minutes rubbing the gelding down with a feed-bag. He put out some hay and made sure there was water for his four legged companion. After washing his hands and face, he went on back up to the house for dinner. He rang the bell once more, not wanting to walk into the house without an invite.

Rue French might well be a thief and a scoundrel, but he did know his manners. In fact, it was one of his trademarks.

"Come on in!" Her voice was strong and steady, and it was clear that there was no nonsense about this woman. She instructed him to come on in to the kitchen, and have a seat. French doffed his hat and looked around as he walked back to where all those wonderful smells were coming from. The place was neat and tidy, and it seemed that books were stacked everywhere. This was a place of learning, and knowledge. Momentarily he forgot his desperate persona, and relished once again to be in the company of well-read folks, folks like himself.

He had no idea who this woman thought he was, but he was totally prepared to be whoever it was she wanted him to be. It would be easy enough to let the conversation take itself wherever it needed to go, and just play the part. It was the kind of thing he excelled at. But walking into the kitchen, Rue French came face to face with his past, in the most unexpected of ways, and here, the most unexpected of places.

There, sitting at the end of the table was a man, an ancient man, with gnarled hands and a face long since grown tired and worn. But the eyes were bright, and burning with life, and the man's voice rang true and clear, a voice French had known so well all those years ago.

"Hello, John. We've been expecting you. Pull up a chair and join us."

The face had changed, older now, much older, but the voice remained the same, strong and steady. French's soul stirred from the memory, the reality of someone who knew him for who he was, for who he had been---before. It was almost more than he could bear, the memories and regrets and heartbreaks held inside for all those years. They would now be laid bare and come out in the open once again--the loss, the betrayal, the very things which had hardened him into the desperate outlaw he had become.

This old man knew it all. This was a moment from which John Cummins could not escape. Here was someone from whom he could not hide using a false identity, a false face, or a false purpose. He thought of running, hiding in the forest, away from these people, running far from this place. But it was for no use.

Instead, he pulled out a chair and sat down. Whatever scheme of Heaven above had brought him to this home, this night, he did not know, but he rightly figured that however uncomfortable this evening might become, it was far better than whatever Heaven might come up with in its place, were he to leave. He knew full well that God Almighty had a potent sense of humor, and that those who failed in His teachings were doomed to be the punch line. He'd stay, and he'd like it.

The old man gave thanks for the food, and a plate of stew and biscuits was placed before the humbled John Cummins. He did not know the woman he had met at the door, having not yet been given introduction, but the man seated to his right was none other than the Reverend Luther Bainer, long time Pastor, and one time friend, who had known John as a child, and had presided at his wedding those many years ago. The beautiful Priscilla had been the Reverend's daughter, and a more amazing bride John Cummins could never have found.

She was a beauty. Men stared and women wilted in her presence. Her smile was disarming, and her voice, soft and lyrical, seemed to comfort the sick or heal the wounded with just a word. This was the woman who had captured the heart of the young John Cummins, a man who was deemed destined for greatness. He had read for the law, and it was suggested that he should run for Congress.

This had all been long ago, long before the war had divided the nation. John still saw Priscilla in his dreams, and whispered her name when he needed comforting, as though she were some spiritual goddess serving as his protector.

But a dashing rival had appeared, handsome and rich and powerful, sweeping the young bride from her senses as the two ran off together to that man's home far away on Cuban shores.

Cummins gave chase, determined to return his beautiful wife to his side, and to vanquish this man and his wanton ways. But the trip proved to be in vain, as the ship which had carried his lovely Priscilla away the week before had vanished in a storm, never to be found. The cruel truth was overwhelming, and John Cummins died as a man, turning instead into a monster--Rue French--a man of wealth, power, and a force to be feared. Emptiness had been filled with more emptiness, until the man known as John Cummins had faded to nothing.

The dinner was delicious, and the light table conversation centered around the weather, the crops, and the general well-being of the nation. Words of anger and mistrust, betrayal and disbelief, had all been spoken out between them long ago. Nothing had been gained, all had been lost. A curse on both their houses.

"How did you know I was coming? I had no idea you were living here. I had believed you to still be back in New York." The matter pressed on Cummins' mind, remembering those who would have him dead, and wondering if perhaps the man sitting next to him might not wish the same. He needed answers.

"Two days ago three men came through this way looking for you. I played ignorant, and as we knew that they were thieves, Martha here shooed them away with that big old horse pistol of hers. They certainly did skedaddle. I'm sorry, I haven't made proper introductions. Martha is our house-keeper, and after Mary died, Martha stayed on here at the manse. The church closed up after the war began, and my rheumatism is so bad now I doubt that I'll ever be able to preach again. It's all I can do to move from one room to the other."

"We buried Mary at the cemetery out behind the church, and I guess I'll be joining her there before too long myself. You'll never know the guilt and shame that haunted Mary all those years over what our Priscilla had done. It made no sense to either of us, as we both knew you had been good to her, and that you loved her. Not having so much as a grave to lay flowers on, made it that much worse. Some folks tried to convince me that a watery grave was what she deserved for her betrayal to you and to our family. I can't accept that, and I never will."

The old man got quiet then, and stared off into the past, nothing left to be said. Martha motioned French to follow her away from the table and back to his room for the night.

"That was the most I've heard him talk for months now. He blames himself for what happened, and he blames himself for what you have become. But it isn't true. You've become who you've become because you're too much of a coward to face the fact that she left you because she wanted to. She was beautiful, yes, but she was selfish and carnal, and the man she ran off with wasn't the first she had seen after you two were married. You were too busy being noble and successful to notice. But others knew, and they should have said something."

It was John Cummins and not Rue French who she was talking to now, and he knew in his heart that her words were true. He had come this far in life clinging to a lie---that he could somehow even the score with the cruelty the world had thrust on him. He had lowered himself into a pit of self-righteous pity, armed with deceit and hatred. And now here he was, fated to sleep once again in a bed that wasn't his, running from those very villains he had helped to create. He was indeed the butt of the joke.

The next morning found French eating a simple breakfast of biscuits with gravy left over from the night before. Two eggs and dark thick coffee rounded out the menu. Once again, it was delicious, but the taste of frustration clouded his soul. The old woman was equal to the moment.

"Follow me out to the cemetery---I'll need your help." As anxious as he was to get back on the trail, Cummins could not in good conscience ignore her request. He calmly waited while she donned her shawl, and then followed her back past the stables, and down a well-worn path toward the little grave-yard behind the long unused church.

The cemetery was overrun with weeds and unraked leaves, a place seldom if ever visited by the families whose loved ones were interred there within the boundaries of the wrought iron fence, itself leaning and bent in disarray. But the dirt path continued through the weeds, showing signs of recent use. And there, in the midst of all of that decay stood a sim-ple stone, beautifully shaped, the ground around it carefully trimmed, with yellow and white flowers growing nearby.

French did not know the names of the flowers, and won-dered at this oasis of care that this stone and its surrounding beauty represented in this desert of weeds. But he was unpre-pared for the letters carved there on the limestone marker, letters that formed a word that he had uttered almost daily over these last many years, the one word that brought him both hope and despair when spoken.

In simple, beautiful script the stone read PRISCILLA. His heart jumped, and his legs weakened. Only had the girl been sitting there awaiting him on her throne could the ef-fect have been more powerful. The man beheld the name of his master, his queen, the goddess who ruled over him every moment of his life. Cummins briefly swooned, and lost his balance, falling clumsily against a stone standing nearby. He tried to collect himself, and fell again, his mind laying pros-trate before a reality greater than himself. The old woman spoke.

"Stay there and rest for a while before you hurt yourself. There can be no greater enemy in this world than ourselves, and for the debt we pay the devil for the privilege of self-pity. You have enjoyed your silliness long enough." She walked over and sat herself down upon the stone itself, this anointed Holy of Holies, as unladylike as though she were sitting on a tree stump.

"She's not here, John. And if she were, what would you do--dig up her bones and hold them close to you like a lover? It doesn't really matter where she lays in death. She was dead to you long before she left you. She did not love you, and she did not love that man she ran off with. You were merely toys, furnishings in her house of self-indulgence. In time she would have cast him aside just the same as she did you. It was you who created her in your own perfect image of womanhood, coveting her beauty, and ignoring her flightiness. Her loss was not your fault, and you did not make her the way she was. And yet you worship her, falling here in anguish at the foot of a stone block marking an empty grave."

John Cummins had not moved his gaze from the name which held him spellbound, and much of what the old woman had said to him had fallen on deaf ears. But she was wise, and filled with the message of truth which was equal to his emptiness.

"Had you come forty years ago I could have made you forget this woman you worship. I had beauty far greater than hers, and I would have captured you and your heart, and held you close to me. I have never been the kind of empty shell of a woman such as the one you married. You remember her loveliness. Hear me now, John Cummins, and save what's left of your life. Women grow young, and then women grow old. How would you have dealt with your precious Priscilla as she aged and decayed as all women do, until she no longer resembled the lovely flower of your youth? Would you have cast her aside, looking away to avoid the sight of her as she aged, and left her sitting alone at home? That is the way of those rich and powerful men who always seem to be surrounded by lovely young women who are eager to trade their beauty for gold and privilege. Would you have been like them?"

John looked up at the old woman, and took a fleeting moment to imagine her as the young beauty that she had claimed to be. The curves were still there, but softened by time, bright eyes on a time-worn face, and once delicate hands now turned thin and spotted. And he looked down at his own hands, hands of a stranger, no longer clear and bold, but scarred and marked, stained with lies, and thievery, and death. The old woman spoke the truth. The Priscilla he longed for was no more alive than the stone which bore her name. He'd been a fool.

John stood himself up, and walked over to this angel of truth.

He held her close to him, kissed her cheek, then turned and walked quickly toward the stables. He was now a new man with a newly found purpose for his life.

His torch was once again raised for Helen Williams. She, and all the other victims of Jacob's self-serving devilment must be avenged! His now was the quest to stamp out the seeds of evil which still lingered among righteous men. A new madness was upon him, the guiding beacon of Priscilla, his reason for living, now darkened. The truth had set his personal devil free, free to be himself once again, now assuming his new identity as John Cummins the avenger.

The evil one must be vanquished. Jacob McPhearson must die.

# CHAPTER THIRTEEN

"**D**o you think you'd know this Rue French fellow if you saw him?" The General was sitting next to Ginny at the kitchen table, enjoying some fresh-brewed tea and warm biscuits with honey. The conversation had centered on the report from Samuel, one of the gardeners, that a man had been making inquiries upstate about the whereabouts of the O'Dell farm. The description of the fellow very closely matched the one that Stronton had used to impersonate French, and rescue Ginny from Judge Bennet's home. The fact that the information had gotten here ahead of the man in question spoke strongly of the unreliable directions he must have received at the time. More than likely given that way on purpose.

Stronton had been expecting this. Sooner or later, the rest of McPhearson's gang were bound to take an interest in this farm, which for so long had been a safe haven for their special brand of devilment. But there was no use running from evil. A man would find it wherever he went. Better to deal with it on your own home turf, where you had the advantage.

Ginny had to think a minute on her father's question. Many men had come and gone at the Judge's house during that last year, and she, along with the other girls had been required to provide 'entertainment' as it were for many of them. This was a shameful time in her young life, and Stronton had hated bringing it up to his daughter like this. But if French's reputation was all that Catherine O'Dell had said it was, it could be a matter of life and death to know who this man was before he were to show up---unannounced.

"I don't believe I ever saw him. I heard the name mentioned, but only once, something about a bank deal up in New England somewhere. But I'm sure the Judge had never met him either, since he thought you were Rue French when you rode in that day. Oh, I wish I could have seen you pull the wool over that old coot's eyes. He always acted nice, but he was really just a cruel old man at heart."

Of course, Stronton wasn't totally in the dark as to French's appearance, having dressed and acted the part of the notorious killer. But he didn't want to be getting so trigger happy as to shoot down every fellow that happened by on a horse just because he might look like the man he was worried about.

"I'll talk more with Samuel, and see if there is anything else he might be able to tell me. It could be we'll need to station someone down at the crossroads for the next few days. He can't be that far off." Stronton was a master strategist, as many a Yankee Commander had painfully discovered. This sort of thing was right up his alley. Excepting of course that now he had his cherished daughter near him again, and he couldn't let anything happen to her, not now, not after all she had been through.

"Daddy, promise me you won't just up and shoot this man when you see him. Talk to him first, and find out how many more there are like him out there. This Mr. French never harmed me. I know how you are sometimes, and you can no more wipe out every man who ever worked for McPhearson than you could the whole Yankee army. I recommend intelligence ahead of action in this case."

Blast it if she hadn't sounded like her mother just then! He really missed Ruthie, and had not known of her death until a month after her burial, given the way he was moving around so frequently toward the end of the war. It was shortly after that when Ginny had been taken. He should have been home. The war was already lost long before then. Lee had been right to fold the flag, even as much as it hurt to do so. It was pride that had kept them fighting, just pride.

Ginny gave her father a gentle peck on the cheek, and went on up to get ready for bed. For some reason the idea of having this dangerous man out there, and heading straight for Dellmont, did not worry her as much as it should. With her father in charge, and all the men he had here to defend them, she knew they would come to no harm. Still, it was very exciting somehow. She just didn't know why she felt that way.

But the General's mind was clouded with doubt, and he did not share his daughter's enthusiasm for the impending arrival of the real Rue French at his doorstep. He sat alone, pondering the possibilities.

The tea suddenly seemed dry, and the biscuits had grown cold.

It was only three days later, and in the early afternoon, that a lone rider wearing tailored clothes approached the main gate of what had once been the home of the O'Dell family, and more recently the stronghold of Jacob McPhearson. There was no doubt in Cummins' mind that this was the right farm. His only concern was just who was living there. He knew McPhearson, and that man would never have wasted time on the kind of niceties he saw before him. Flowering plants were carefully planted around the entrance, and over the newly-installed gateway were large letters announcing the place as 'DELLMONT'. The iron work was new and had not been there before. Something had happened here, and he got the distinct and immediate impression that whoever it was that was running the show around here now, Jacob McPhearson was not that man.

Cummins remembered being at this farm before, near nightfall it was, and recalled thinking what a nice little place it could be if Jacob would bother fixing it up a bit. But Jacob had no eye for beauty, only lust for whatever was not yet his. Cummins often wondered how he ever got mixed up with such a man in the first place.

Still, he needed information. And he needed to find Jacob, and settle the score. He rode in, carefully, slowly. Soon the house came into view, white, with green shutters, and flowers and plants everywhere. The place seemed otherwise deserted, excepting for an older gentleman wearing a white suit coat, and rocking in a chair on the freshly painted porch. He looked for all the world like the perfect country gentleman sitting in the afternoon shade, just watching the world go by. Cummins' observations couldn't have been more wrong.

In that chair sat former Brigadier General James Stronton, late of the Army of Virginia, and unknown to Cummins, the cause of all the trouble that had followed him since New York. Also unknown to him was that the peaceful looking General had his very lethal LeMat pistol out and hidden under a pillow, pointing in the visitor's direction. That very pistol had already dispatched more than a few of Jacob McPhearson's unfortunate associates, and was quite capable of adding another to the tally. John rode ahead cautiously. Stronton sat patiently. The imposter awaited the pretender.

When Cummins got within twenty feet of the porch, Stronton stood up, and in the manner of a duelist, pointed his lethal looking LeMat unerringly at the chest of his uninvited visitor.

"I have a very good idea who you are, and just what it is you are doing here. If I'm right, I have every reason to go ahead and shoot you now and get it over with. I will advise you, sir, that there are three rifles trained on you at this moment, one above and one on either side of you. I would go ahead and kill you now, except that I have promised to let you speak your piece first. Please remove your weapons very slowly, and throw them behind your horse." Stronton was speaking softly, but the darkness in his face belayed any thoughts that this was a soft spoken man. John's words came as a surprise.

"I'm sorry, sir. I can't do that. I might get by with the rifle, which as you can see is safely in its scabbard. But this pistol is very touchy, and were I to drop it, there is every chance that it would go off on its own accord. The bullet might hit my horse, and this is too good a horse to be shot in the rear. It just wouldn't be right. I would, however, hand it to you slowly, grip first, if you wish. I came here for information, not for a fight, and I need no weapons to talk." Cummins hadn't moved, and his expression hadn't changed. Stronton smiled a bit at this man's grit, and decided not to make things any worse.

"Very well then. Please get down slowly, and hand your pistol to me after you've dismounted." French followed the man's instructions as asked, pulling his pistol very slowly from his shoulder holster with the weight of the General's LeMat firmly against his spine. He then removed his hat and his coat, and allowed himself to be thoroughly searched by one of Stronton's men who came up from behind--a fourth rifle not previously mentioned.

Stronton then led the visitor over to an adjacent chair on the porch, while the man's horse was led away to the stables. Cummins started to complain, but decided to just sit and be quiet instead. In many ways, the man seated next to him was far more dangerous than Jacob McPhearson could ever be.

Cummins knew McPhearson for the murdering skunk he was. But he was known to have a mean streak about him that always wanted to terrorize his victims before he did them in. In comparison, this gentleman was simply one who had killed before and would kill again, especially if he thought it needed to be done. Cummins knew he was closer to being dead right at that moment than he had been at any time previous in his life---and that covered a lot of ground.

"You are in fact the man known as Rue French. And you have come here today to meet with Jacob McPhearson. So, as I refuse to spend time speaking with dishonest men, you will please tell me your true name, so that we may continue our visit. That, or I can treat you as the criminal that you are, and I will end this conversation right here and now." The LeMat had not wavered. Neither did the visitor.

"You are correct sir. I am known by the name of Rue French, and by many other names as well, as the need arises. But my Christian name is John Cummins, and my being here has very much to do with my need to regain my true identity, and perhaps a bit of my lost honor, if there be any left." There it was. He had not said his name out loud to any other human being for more years than he could remember. He had come to this place to rid himself of his partnership with Jacob McPhearson. It seemed he was going to first be forced to rid himself of himself.

# CHAPTER FOURTEEN

Stronton looked deeply into the eyes of John Cummins, alias Rue French, and saw a very determined man with great courage. Boldness comes from audacity and pride, often a bad combination. But courage comes from deep inside. The man sitting next to him had courage. He had stood his ground, and came looking for something that he had to deal with--his past, and maybe his future.

"So tell me sir, why have you come here today? What is your purpose for seeking out this place? What is your business here?"

"I have come to find and to kill Jacob McPhearson, my former associate, and a man who has apparently put a death mark out on me, and at a high rate of exchange. Perhaps you could help me to know where he has gone, as it is clear to me that he is no longer here in this beautiful place. I need to find him quickly. My life depends on it." Cummins' eyes held steady.

"Mr. Cummins, I am James Stronton, formerly Brigadier with the Army of Virginia. As for Jacob McPhearson, your questions will be answered in good time. But first, sir, tell me, what was your role during the recent conflict?" The LeMat still had not wavered, and Cummins knew he was in a difficult position. But he had decided days before to end the lies, and he made good here as well.

"I fought only for myself, and the cheap gains I could enjoy from the stupidity of others. I have been a swindler, and a thief, and a fool. But I have never killed a man who didn't have it coming, or wasn't gunning for me first. In recent days I have been running from men who I once knew as associates, who are now bent on killing me on sight, as there is that price on my head. I have come to this place seeking McPhearson, the man who I assume has put this bounty on me, for reasons I do not know. I came here seeking him as I know that he had been running opium and slaves from this very farm for some time. I myself visited this place over a year ago, while he was still my partner. I am exactly who you think I am. And ridding this world of Jacob is the first step in restoring my honor as a man."

This then was indeed the genuine Rue French, the very man that Stronton had impersonated, using Catherine O'Dell's descriptions. She had been amazingly accurate, and the General felt a chill run up his spine as he realized that the man sitting beside him might well be as truly ruthless and dangerous as Catherine had said.

"Mr. Cummins, I still have not decided whether or not to shoot you, but as you are being forthright with me, I will do the same by you. I owe you that much. But first, please allow me to offer you some refreshment. The day is getting warmer, and my glass has fallen empty. And of course, it is bad manners to drink alone. Ginny! Please bring us two more cups of that mint tea, and some of those sweet cakes you made up yesterday." Cummins was fully expecting some brown-skinned matron to be bringing out a tray of refreshments. Old habits would die hard in the South. Ginny's appearance took him totally by surprise.

The girl came lightly through the porch door, expertly balancing a wooden tray with three cups, along with a plate of sweet cakes cut into squares and dusted with fine sugar. She moved with an agility and grace honed by her time as a servant girl in the home of Judge Bennet.

Cummins watched as the lovely young girl with the long dark hair deftly placed the tray on the table between them, and carefully handed a glass of tea to each of the men. She then lifted the third cup, and helping herself to a sweet bread, took a seat in a rocking chair nearby. The whole thing had been a set up. If Stronton had asked for sandwiches, Ginny would have come out a different door and placed a gun at the back of Cummins' head. The sweet breads meant that things were under control. Stronton had left nothing to chance.

"Mr. Cummins, this is my daughter Ginny. Tell me Ginny, do you know this man, or have you ever seen him before?" The girl had already been looking this fellow over, and was quickly convinced she did not know him.

"No, Daddy. This man is very handsome, and quite dashing. His is a face that no woman would be likely to forget. I've never met him." Cummins didn't quite know what to make of this inspection, but wisely decided to hold off any comment until he could find out just where all this was going. She certainly was pretty.

"Mr. Cummins, or Mr. French, whoever you are, my daughter here was one of the many girls who were kidnapped and imprisoned by your partner Jacob McPhearson during these last several years, and were in turn sold as white slaves to unscrupulous men both here and abroad. It pleases me to inform you that Jacob is dead and buried on the plains of Kansas, shot down while in the act of attacking his own niece. This farm has been given to us by surviving members of the O'Dell family, and so we are here today. McPhearson's trash who had infested this place were dealt with, and I assure you they will not be seen in these parts again."

Things had changed--drastically. McPhearson would never allow these things to happen if he were alive. Kansas? That made no sense, but the tale of him attacking his niece rang true to what he knew of the man. French had met Catherine O'Dell at this very farm, but only in passing. He knew her to be Jacob's niece, and remembered her being very pretty and very bright, with eyes that seemed to see everything. He recalled her being very mysterious and distant, almost foreign in many ways. She was the kind of girl that would bring out the animal stupidity that Jacob was known for. If this man said that Jacob was dead, he would accept the facts as given until informed otherwise. Stronton continued.

"I think you should also know that on the advice of Miss O'Dell, I assumed your identity as Rue French, and visited the offices of Judge Bennet in Richmond, using falsified papers and an invented story, to rescue my daughter from the Judge's household. A few days later I led a group of volunteers against this farm to wipe out McPhearson's nest of evil which resided here, and in the process rescued a girl who was living here in chains. At the same time another group under my command entered the Judge's home in Richmond, and dealing with his thugs, freed the other stolen girls that had lived there with Ginny, and then burned the place to the ground. The Judge was later found hanging by the neck in his own office with a suicide note nearby, implicating other members of Jacob's organization, thus freeing more girls. It is unlikely that the girls who were smuggled overseas will ever be recovered." Stronton sat silent then and allowed all this information to sink in. He watched as the brave countenance of Rue French dissolved into the pained features of John Cummins.

"After what he had done..." The last words of Chet Gillen now made more sense than before. If those who survived thought that it had been Rue French who had carried out those raids, it would have been more than enough to justify a death mark upon him. But if Jacob and the Judge were indeed dead, who then could be running the show? He was more at a loss than before. It made no sense. Still, he had a responsibility to this young woman. A debt he could never repay.

"I am truly sorry. I had nothing to do with that part of Jacob's business. I've never done anything to anyone who wasn't in one way or another asking for it. I was aware of much of what Jacob was doing, but I turned a blind eye to it all. This is a past which I must somehow help to put an end to. Seeing your daughter here so pretty and fresh and bright, brings shame to me that I had been a part of Jacob's dealings. I ran drugs and money and collected debts. I did the dirty jobs he gave me, along with my own. I suppose I never really thought about the rest of it all. I am terribly sorry." Cummins sat quietly then, and looked down at his hands, hands that had so often dealt cards faster than the eye could follow. Hands stained with blood that would never come clean. Ginny broke the silence, and spoke her mind in a clear and steady voice.

"Mr. Cummins, I'm going to tell you in great detail what your partner did to me, because I want you to know the whole truth, and I want you to understand why I might shoot you myself before this day is over, and I promise I would take my sweet time in doing it."

Stronton had not planned on this, but seeing the hurt in his daughter's eyes, he decided it might be best for her to get this all out in the open. But he would draw the line at her shooting this man. He wasn't about to let her live on with that sort of thing on her conscience. He would do that himself.

Ginny's story was direct, to the point, and sickening. She described the events of her capture and imprisonment in detail. She looked the man known as Rue French square in the eye as she recalled her life as a concubine, living there in the heart of Richmond, with no means of escape. She spoke of the other girls she had known, some for only a day or two, and some who she had seen tortured, beaten, and murdered by the Judge's men. Her memories were clear, and terrible.

She also mentioned meeting Catherine O'Dell, the spirited young woman who had once called this place home, and presumably the one responsible for Jacob McPhearson's death. Ginny smiled at the memory, and wished she had known her better.

The General sat and listened, tears welling in his eyes. This was the first time Ginny had spoken at length of her imprisonment since her rescue, and here she was telling it all to a total stranger. But Stronton had seen grief and guilt before, and knew that sometimes talking it out was the best way to rid the demons.

The day went on, the conversation moving on to more common topics, and shared experiences. After a time Ginny excused herself and went back inside. At the General's insistence, the two men got up and walked along the grounds, admiring the finely bred horses, the newly rebuilt stables, and the splendor of the forests and mountains which could be seen in the distance. When they finally got back to the house, the men renewed their conversation out on the porch, enjoying the evening air and the pleasant scent of the newly planted flowers nearby. Stronton cleared his throat signaling the difficulty he was having in finding the words to say that which he was honor bound to say. He didn't much like it, but he had no choice in the matter.

"Mr. Cummins, the day is getting late. And as strange as it may seem, I am obliged to offer you a place to stay for the night. Please accept this invitation to be our guest until morning." The General didn't much like making the offer, but a Southern Gentleman has certain obligations to his guests, even to those who are scoundrels and enemies.

John considered the General's offer, knowing full well that it was given solely from duty and not affection. But even if it had been, he felt that he had already caused these folks enough grief, if only because of the people he had so foolishly associated with. No, he had overstayed any welcome he might have ever been given here, and seeing how he was still alive and breathing, he figured that a night out on the trail would be far better than a bullet. He decided to decline the offer.

And he was about to do just that, when out through the front door came the lovely young Ginny brandishing a very evil looking shotgun with a determined look on her face that would have put any block of granite to shame.

"Mr. Cummins, I know what you're thinking, and if you think you're going to be getting out of here that easily and ride off to who knows where to do who knows what, well you have another thing to think. I have fixed a fine supper and you will come in this minute and set yourself up at the table and eat your fill, and then accept my father's offer to stay the night. If you dare to refuse our hospitality, I will consider you to be the very varmint everyone says you are and shoot you where you stand right here and now." The determined look had not left her face, and her aim was right for his midsection. Cummins decided that a belly full of her cooking, good or bad, would set far and away better than a belly full of lead from that shotgun. And he knew she meant it.

"General Stronton, I would be delighted to accept your offer to stay the night, and I am looking forward to the meal that Ginny here has prepared. It seems that your daughter is a most persuasive hostess."

"That she is, Mr. Cummins. She got that from her mother."

# CHAPTER FIFTEEN

D inner was simple but elegant, and Cummins was very glad that he had been persuaded to partake, even if it had been with a shotgun-laced invitation. Would she have actually shot him? Well, the slighted invitation to a dinner such as this would probably be grounds enough, all things considered. It certainly did trump the sorry offerings he carried in his saddle bags.

"Miss Stronton, I thank you for inviting me in for this delicious dinner. I can't recall when I last sat down to a meal like this, and in such lovely company." With that, Cummins almost choked. It was the standard harmless flirtation he had plied on more than one hostess in his day, not necessarily expecting any sort of special consideration for his words.

But here he had thoughtlessly complemented a young woman's lovely appearance, while she had only recently been abducted, enslaved, and ravaged by men who thought of her only as a toy to be played with, with no consideration for her in the least. He needed to be more careful when he spoke, whether he meant it or not.

"I thank you for your kindness, Mr. Cummins. We don't often get the chance to entertain guests here, and while you have behaved in the past as a most vicious and underhanded killer, I am pleased that you have presented yourself as a courteous and learned gentleman this evening. So tell me sir, where did you receive your schooling? You seem very well read." The sideways smile on her face was more powerful than the shotgun she had been wielding earlier, and twice as lethal. This was no mere babe in the woods. It seemed that Cummins had been running into a great many overly wise women as of late, young and old, and apparently he was no longer up for the challenge. It was embarrassing.

"You are too kind, Miss Stronton, I have never thought of myself as a scholar in any way whatsoever, but I have had the privilege of reading from among the best of the authors of our time, and from the classics as well. I will in fact gladly give all credit for any such knowledge to my own dear mother, who raised me with a stick in her right hand and a book in her left. I suppose I have always been curious about the world around me, and of the ways of men and nations."

"And yet you chose not to put your skills to use in the recent conflict." General Stronton had been sitting off in the corner, gun at ready but no longer drawn, listening with interest to his daughter as she took this stranger to task. He couldn't help but notice how she seemed to come alive with the challenge of this, her distant tormentor being here at her doorstep. Yet the man's refusal to fight in a war with so much at stake left a bad taste in the General's mouth. And he had sat back and been silent about it long enough.

"You are correct sir, I did not. It was mindless slaughter on both sides, with men marching in columns straight into cannons and mini-balls fired to tear them to pieces. We do better when we slaughter cattle. And here we are, five years later with nothing to show for it. An entire generation has been wiped out while rich men got richer selling the weapons they used to kill one another. And now we are killing the natives out west with equal enthusiasm to satisfy our desires for land and riches. I like none of it, and I did not join into the insanity just to become another dead man in a uniform. Your daughter is right, I am a scoundrel, and I have killed, but the men I killed brought the fight to me, and they were all armed and willing to do me harm. I never ordered a rifle brigade to fire into a group of men willy-nilly, to end the lives of drummer boys and flag bearers. There is no glory in such a war."

Cummins stopped talking then. He looked down at the floor knowing full well he had said too much, and with a fervor and wrath unbefitting his place as a guest in this man's home. But he had lied long enough, about himself, his feelings, and his own identity as well. At that moment he knew the truth---Rue French must die---die and be dead forever. His name was John Cummins, and if this Confederate General was of a mind to shoot him dead, then fine, have it over with. But he would die as himself, John Cummins, with the trappings of his loathsome past behind him.

"I'm afraid your words hold truth, young man. Sitting here now, with the echoes of the dead and dying still ringing in my ears, I can no longer summon up the words I would need to argue the point. When you arrived here today I was quite prepared to shoot you down where you stood, on account of the harm I believed you had done to my daughter by being associated with Jacob McPhearson and his like. I was holding you responsible not for the things you have done, but rather for the things your associates have done. And the matter of whether or not you willingly condone the actions of others by knowingly joining their ranks is a discussion yet to be decided. But hearing your words, spoken in earnest, has given me pause in my thinking." The General was struggling with his thoughts here.

"I myself have been responsible for the deaths of many a fine young soldier, Yankee and Confederate alike, men who will never go home to see their wives or their mothers, while I tried to hold on to a cause that we long before knew was lost. The man who once owned this farm, William O'Dell, fell at Shiloh, which began a series of events that now finds us sitting here today discussing his death along with thousands of others. As a promise to his daughter, I placed a marker out in the family plot in that man's honor, and yet his body lies somewhere else, on a battlefield far away. These things are troubling to think on. I wish to speak no more about it today, perhaps another time." The General then smiled, thoughtfully.

"Would you instead share a glass of brandy with me, Mr. Cummins? --- a toast between two killers of men, here today by the grace of God, to enjoy the fresh air and the joys of creation. And may fate smile upon us that we can somehow live to make our tomorrows better than our yesterdays." Cummins had looked this man in the eye as he had spoken, from the heart, from the soul, and nodded in silent agreement to the truth of the General's words. There was a bond between them here, not of friendship, or even respect, but of the heavy weight of responsibility that falls on those who survived, those who somehow had not died in the carnage.

Ginny had been listening intently to these two men as they had fenced and parried with words, and had emptied their hearts to one another. She poured the brandy and handed out the glasses. This night her world had changed. She now saw her valiant father in a whole new light, subdued, and regretful. And this man called Rue French, who had been a compatriot of the vicious Jacob McPhearson, had proved to be nothing more than a brilliant man with a conscience, who had compromised himself to make a quick dollar. Still, she sensed there was more to him than she knew --- much more.

And here she was now, judging others, but with a scarlet past of her own, some of which she knew she had from time to time secretly enjoyed, and much too much of which she had shared openly with this handsome stranger, wanting him to know, wanting him to understand, wanting him to...

No, she mustn't think those things. This man was very handsome, and bright and charming and dashing! It was almost like having some swashbuckling adventurer right there among them, and staying over as a house guest of all things! He was dangerous --- and he was wonderful.

None of them slept well that night, but the feather beds were surely not to blame. Nor was the moon, which hid itself behind the clouds, or the owl which fell silent early, while a soft breeze rustled in the trees nearby.

Cummins found himself in a peculiar spot. Staying the night in the home of a stranger was not that uncommon for him, although he would usually be hiding behind some alias or other while he was there. He had expected to find

McPhearson here. He had built himself up for that confrontation for the better part of a month now. It seemed impossible that the man could be dead, and laying in some unmarked grave out on the Kansas prairie. It wasn't fair.

He had come here to end Jacob's life by his own hand, to avenge his honor, and respond in kind to the death mark he had believed that man had placed upon him. Furthermore, it had been his promised duty to gun down the man who had taken advantage of the young and innocent Helen Williams, leaving her alone with child. He was to be Helen's champion, slaying her personal dragon --- reaping vengeance!

Along with Jacob's death came questions. If McPhearson hadn't been the one to set that death mark upon him, then who did? Or rather, who could? Who would have the power in McPhearson's organization to do such a thing? The Judge was dead as well. What was he missing here? Who should he then be looking for? It was a worrisome thing.

If all that weren't enough, the man of this house, a retired General of all things, had been prepared to shoot him on sight. While he had somehow escaped that unhappy event so far, the man still had that look in his eye from time to time. While he might have to stay around a few days to convince them he was harmless and to arrange his get away, the sooner he left the better would be his chance to stay alive.

The whole thing would have been difficult enough if it weren't for the girl. Ginny Stronton was lovely, and spirited, and different from any woman he'd ever met before. She was young, and yet wise in the ways of a woman. He figured himself to be somewhere near twice her age, but didn't seem to feel that difference when they were together. He was thinking nonsense now, and saw no way the two of them could ever...

At last his weary body had given in, even as his cluttered mind continued its whirlwind of thought. Sleep softly overtook him, while sitting up in a chair, his boots still on his feet. John Cummins had been ambushed after all, the victim of the beauty of a place called Dellmont, and of the amazing young woman who called this place home.

John Cummins stayed that night, and the next, and the next. He and Stronton stayed busy riding on horseback around the estate and into the hills beyond. John marveled at the lush pastures, the newly acquired cattle, and the many building projects underway, some for storage, some for water control, and a fine looking row of houses for those men who worked there on the estate. Some had come with their families, and very little else. They would now share in the wonder of this place called Dellmont.

The men spoke openly and honestly together, with Cummins sharing tales of his many narrow escapes from desperate killers, and the General going on and on with tales of the war, and of strategies used ---some that worked, some that didn't.

This was a good time for both men, a chance to get much of the torment of their former lives out in the open. And in doing so, a trust was built between them, brought forth by the need for closure. It was an unlikely pairing, but solid.

In the same light, Cummins found himself accompanying young Ginny on daily rides around the estate as well, her riding skills on display. She took great interest in this man and his knowledge of things. They would often stop and talk for hours, sharing their thoughts and dreams. These rides became the highlight of their days together, and with a kind of closeness neither one had ever felt before. Smile welcomed smile, and soon their whole world had changed right before their eyes, and in a manner that neither of them could have ever imagined.

It was on one such ride that Ginny learned of John's reading for the law, and of his betrothal to Priscilla. He had felt it safe to open his heart, and to bare his soul to Ginny. This was a kind of trust that he had never experienced before, not with anyone.

He spoke freely, and allowed years of torment and betrayal to be released, to be confessed, to be known by someone other than himself ---someone he trusted, someone he cared for. She responded with a woman's wisdom---far beyond her years.

"Mr. Cummins, I hear the hurt in your voice, just as you have no doubt heard the hurt in mine these last many days. I felt betrayed by Heaven above for what happened to me, and yet, I was blessed by that same Heaven, as my father somehow found me, and brought me safe to this wonderful place. I struggle to understand it all."

"You're right, Ginny. I know I've felt that same betrayal, but I had taken another path and tried somehow to get even by doing as much damage as possible. And I did. I am ashamed of who I've become. Oddly enough, I am a wealthy man, with money scattered in banks all across the northern states."

"And yet, I have nothing. I don't have a house of my own, or even a bed of my own to sleep in. In many ways I am the poorest of men. I would like to change all of that, but I don't know how, not with the reputation I have built for myself.

Maybe I could go west, and start over, somehow. But I know in my heart that running away isn't the answer. There will always be someone, somewhere who will remember me for who I was. Can you understand what I'm saying?" Ginny had been watching this man's eyes, honest eyes, sincere eyes, full of regret. She spoke from her heart in return.

"Yes, John, I understand all too well, perhaps more than you could ever know. While I was captive, I was forced to be with many men. They have touched me, and seen me, and used me. I know for certain that many of those same men are still out there, some in business, and some in the government. The Judge only entertained important people, and rich people with power. When those same men see me on the street one day, or at church, or at the fair, what will they do --- what will they say? Will they shame me in whispers to their friends? Will they brazenly approach me, expecting me to do their bidding in return for keeping my secret? Will they try to blackmail my father to maintain their silence?"

"I agree, sir, running is not the answer. Sooner or later someone will know me, will remember me for what I have done, and the gossips will flourish. It is a thing that will follow me everywhere that I go, just as those things will follow you. Our only choice is to live on, and to live as well as the world will allow, or not to live at all. I will not give up my life because of what others have done to me. I will live on, no matter what."

There was, in fact, a resigned attraction which had grown between the two of them. Both felt a longing for the chance for true love, long ago lost, but so very much needed. But neither of them had been willing to let go of their fears and sorrows, the darkness which they each held close, the torment which they were afraid to leave behind.

It was this fear of their pasts which had somehow become their identity, shaping their emptiness and solitude. And it was their new-found trust in one another which broke that spell. True love had opened the door.

Then it happened. It was just a brush of an arm, the rustle of fabric upon soft skin, and suddenly she was in his arms, clinging, desperately holding on to the promise of acceptance, of trust, of understanding.

No words were spoken, and yet the questioning continued. They found their answers in each other's arms, an embrace which broke the spell of evil which had separated them from a love unreachable, unfindable, and unallowed.

An hour or so later they finally returned, two people with souls newly quieted, but for very different reasons. John Cummins helped the lovely young lady dismount, and taking the reins, led the horses to the stables, while Ginny walked slowly up to the house. Suddenly she turned back, and ran back to her new and closest friend, born together as one, and paired as only Heaven, or the fates, could arrange.

"Please, John, once more." She pressed her lips against his, wanting once more to feel the promise of love and acceptance, to once again be the woman she had dreamed so long of becoming.

Cummins closed his eyes and relished in the perfume of the moment, suddenly alive, and curiously happy. He watched her go up to the porch and back into the house, happily humming a tune, and once again joyful in life.

But as Cummins walked the horses on back to the stables, he was somehow unaware of the lone figure which stood nearby in the shadows. Those eyes had seen what had become of the two of them, and his heart grew hot with hatred because of it.

Stronton had seen the kiss, and he knew the rest. It seemed that Rue French had come to exact his price for Ginny's freedom after all, that price being Ginny herself. The General's hand rested anxiously upon the revolver hanging by his side. Not here, not now.

He should have shot him dead the first moment he saw him.

# CHAPTER SIXTEEN

That evening's dinner was awkwardly quiet, the usual banter between the three of them having been replaced with downcast eyes and far away glances. Ginny and John had much to talk about, each building a list of wishes for their future in each other's company. But those words were to remain unspoken, as the presence of the girl's father, his eyes now serious and piercing, precluded all careless talk---an irritation for the girl, and a warning for caution which was not lost on the older and wiser Cummins.

Having eaten quickly and quietly, the General excused himself early from the meal, and went back to his room for the night. His mind was set, and there were things that needed to be done, details to be covered, a mission to complete.

Stronton slowly removed the trusty LeMat pistol from its holster. This weapon had been his companion and protector on countless fields of battle in years past, an extension of himself as it were, and now the partner that would be called upon to complete the task at hand. He carefully cleaned and oiled the gun, knowing full well that going up against a man with the kind of reputation that the name Rue French brought to mind would leave no room for error. No matter their recent cordial relationship, John Cummins, or Rue French, as it were, would not be allowed to destroy his daughter's life. That man's association with the likes of Jacob McPhearson told Stronton everything he had needed to know from the beginning. The fact that Cummins had nearly won his trust was merely a testimony to the skills and cunning that man possessed.

This was a challenge that Stronton would have to meet head on, a task that would require expert marksmanship, cold steel nerves, and a weapon that would not hesitate to deliver when called upon. He took as much care with the reloading as he had with the cleaning. Plans were made over a stiff glass of fine brandy. The matter would be settled tomorrow, or the next day at the latest. Maybe a staged hunting accident...

Stronton listened carefully as first his daughter, and then his house guest, made their way down the hallway and into their rooms for the night. His blood boiled as he visualized the goodnight kiss and embrace that must have closed their evening together. Cummins was taking advantage of Ginny's need for affection and acceptance. His methods were all too obvious. The General would need a second shot of brandy that night to settle his nerves enough for bed. He would need yet another to allow him to catch up with his fitful and elusive sleep.

Somewhere in the night Stronton was awakened by the soft patter of feet on the newly polished oak floors. He angrily arose from his slumber, anxious to catch the black-guard Cummins in the act, callously ravaging his young and vulnerable daughter as she slumbered.

He crept down the hallway and carefully opened Ginny's door, expecting to find the unthinkable, there under his own roof. But all he found was a girl safe in bed, covers drawn to her chin, the moon shining in on the very sight he had prayed so long to be true---his daughter safe at home, and nearby once again.

Stronton went back to his bed, angry, confused, and embarrassed. The little girl he had left behind when the war began, the one he had searched desperately to find, was no longer there. That little girl was now a woman, so much like her mother. He could not deny what he knew. He was losing the most precious thing in his life to the most clever of thieves, one being Rue French, the other, time itself.

One he would kill quickly, and without mercy. The other had beaten him already.


John Cummins thrashed and turned through the night, haunted by a vision that would not be satisfied: the lovely face of Ginny Stronton, innocent and helpless, bound as a captive, and unable to free herself from those who tormented her, beckoned for his aid, his help in ending her torment. He had to save her, somehow to reach her and free her from that bondage. The dream played itself out over and over again, and even when awake, the vision would not clear itself from his mind.

She had told him of her greatest fear, that someone some-day would recognize her, and that she would be known and ridiculed in polite society, bringing shame upon her father, and living her life in a prison of fear and humiliation.

His devotion for this girl had gone unchecked, his need for her now undeniable. The headstone over the empty grave had brought to light the truth about Priscilla, a truth he hadn't wanted to believe, a truth he hadn't been willing to accept---the truth about himself.

But now came Ginny, spirited, sincere, and needing his protection from the very world she must now somehow re-enter. Her happiness was in his hands---and his happiness was with her.

She was lovely, and her passion, and love for life was surely all that he could ever ask, and more than he had ever known before. But he knew that her fears would cast a shadow over their happiness together, and it was up to him to calm those waters once and for all. And so, like a knight in days of old, John Cummins would take up his sword, and go into battle to protect his lady, her virtue, and her life. His life now had purpose.

It was not quite sunup when John Cummins, his thoughts finally collected, stood up from his bed, and quickly dressing, walked softly down the stairs and out to the stables. Within minutes he was gone.

He could have waited, he could have tried to say goodbye. But she would have asked him to stay, and wept when he refused, and he would have been forced to ride away without her blessing. No, it was better this way, her trust in him never failing, waiting faithfully for his return, and then rejoicing in his triumph over her foes.

He would go to Richmond, and avenge the fair Ginny Stronton, laying waste to those who had defiled her lovely countenance, and giving back her lost innocence, and pride. There would be no one left to speak wrong of her. He would ride into hell to free her soul from torment. His life was now forfeit, serving only as her avenger, and her champion. His guilt would not permit him to fail, for of all men, his was the burden to right the wrong that his foolishness had helped to create. The skills of Rue French were now bound to the honor of John Cummins---a new and dangerous scourge for any who stood before him.

Henry Stronton had been awakened once again as he heard footsteps walking softly down the stairway. He watched from hiding as his guest rode out of the stables, through the gate, and out to the road beyond. Cummins' leaving was un-expected, but not out of character---the thief skulking away in the darkness.

Stronton was certain that Ginny knew nothing of this early morning departure--she would never have permitted it. Ginny had fallen in love with this dashing highwayman, who would break her heart just as all those of his kind were so well known to do. But for Stronton the man's behavior was surely a breach of trust, the fleecing of an innocent, regardless of her invitations and unwelcomed past. This then was an af-front and would not go unpunished. Yet another reason for Stronton to end John Cummins' life.

But he would not meet this man on the field of honor, for this man had no honor. The General would simply hunt him down like the animal he was, and end the legend of Rue French once and for all. The matter was decided.

Stronton turned from his window and began dressing. Whatever sleep he would be getting that night was already behind him. Better to be up and moving than to thrash uselessly in bed. He'd done enough of that already this night.

But John Cummins' departure had been witnessed by a second man as well, a man known there at Dellmont simply as Layland. He worked in the stables and made it his task to see and hear everything which went on around him. He had learned of the General's raid on the Judge's offices, and had recognized the real Rue French from a time years before, back to when he had lived up north. The events of these last few days were as confusing as they were useful. Information like this could be worth a great deal to the right man, the man that Layland served in secret.

That man was Jacques Benine, the true leader of the gang which had put Ginny Stronton in chains, the man who had put the death mark on Rue French, and who had been running the evil cartel for years. Benine was the man that Stronton had known only as Judge Bennet's butler. Jacques Benine had hidden right out in the open. The butler had gone unaccounted for as the General's men swept through the Judge's stronghold in a bold effort to eliminate that scum from the earth. That operation had not been as successful as Stronton had been led to believe.

A few minutes after Cummins had cleared the gate, Layland was also on horseback, but headed south and west, to the stronghold of Jacques and his den of thieves, eager to sell the information he had gathered, as well as the horse he had stolen as he left Dellmont that morning. When evil goes unchecked, it survives and grows like poison ivy. But its itch is far more devastating.

# CHAPTER SEVENTEEN

G inny came down for breakfast that morning an hour or so later than usual. She found her father sitting in a rocking chair out on the porch, puffing thoughtfully on his pipe, and looking off into the distance at nothing in particular. She had expected to see John Cummins sitting there too, but he was not to be found. There was a chill in the air, just as there had been the morning before, and the morning before that. With a blanket wrapped around his legs and his dark hair beginning to turn white, she saw her father now as the man he had become, not the man she had known as a child. The war had aged him. It would be a hard thing to get used to.

"He's gone, Ginny, rode out before first light. Made no effort to say goodbye. In fact, he snuck out like he wanted to make sure we didn't see him go. I would have thought better of the man, but I guess that's just who he is after all."

Ginny walked over and took her father's hand, holding it in hers, close to her. Tears fell, as much for herself as for the man who had ridden away.

"He would have at least thanked us for our hospitality and said goodbye, unless of course he knew he'd be back before long. He probably just wanted to let me sleep in. He's very considerate of others that way, in fact he reminds me of you sometimes. I think I understand better now why Mother chose you, and the sort of frustration living with a man like you can bring." Ginny's words fell on the General's ears in a way he had never heard them before. His resolve was beginning to wane as he understood just how deep her relationship with Cummins had grown, and how well they had come to know one another. He tried to recover with a new train of thought.

"The man who arrived here a few days ago was not the same man we came to know while he was here, and I fear not the same man once again who rode out this morning. I think that his being here was a lesson for all three of us, a lesson and a warning as well. Last year's regrets are as unfit for us to partake as is last year's food. We'll all either live our lives fresh every day, or we will surely be poisoned by what lays behind us. He was here, and now he's gone. This was his choice. This is his way. It's best that you let him stay gone." He patted Ginny's hand and hoped his words had made a difference.

"You don't think we'll ever see him again, do you Daddy? You think he'll just keep going and never come back. This is what you want, isn't it?" The General looked up at his daughter's angry face and realized he had said too much. It was time to tell the truth as he knew it.

"The man who rode out of here this morning will never be back, Ginny. It's probably best that way. But if he does come back, we'll once again give him the chance to speak his piece, and explain himself. But remember, what he did once he'll most likely do again." The General thought for a moment, and then decided that this conversation needed to be put to rest. Enough already.

"But I can't be waiting for my breakfast while we talk about all of this. John Cummins might or might not be coming back, but there's a good chance he won't be back in time for breakfast, and I'm hungry. We'll talk about this later, and maybe make some kind of sense of it. In the meantime, why don't you run into the kitchen and see if you can rustle up some flapjacks. I swear girl you make flapjacks as good as your mother did." With that a smile found its way back to Ginny's face, the debate being temporarily over. Soon enough she was humming a tune and tapping on the table top with a wooden spoon to keep the beat.

Stronton had heard her humming like that a lot these last few days. The Ginny he had known before was home again. He knew now for certain that she had fallen in love with that scoundrel, and that he now filled a place in her heart that another evil man had emptied out against her will. He wondered at the irony of it all. He unwillingly found himself questioning his motives for wanting John Cummins dead.

Soon the wonderful smell of hotcakes filled the air, and he knew that she would be calling him in to breakfast at any moment. He wanted nothing but happiness for his daughter, but he was certain that whatever love she felt for that man was seated in her desperation for affection, and a cure for her loneliness. He couldn't let her become lost again so soon after getting her back again. He somehow had to find a way to make her see the danger of what she was doing, to rethink the way she felt for this man. It was his fatherly duty to stop this travesty before it went any further. His gun was ready and waiting. There was only one solution here.

Rue French must die.

# CHAPTER EIGHTEEN

Jacques Benine sat comfortably on a large overly padded parlor chair, looking down upon the man who lay kneeling on the floor below him. The visage could not have been that much different from that of a medieval potentate holding court, while some unfortunate subordinate or other prostrated himself in hopes of avoiding his majesty's wrath. This man, known only as Layland, had authored his own misfortune by the bringing of bad news, some of which was not flattering to his lordship, Jacques.

The throne room parallels ended with the furnishings, opulent and beautiful as they may have been. Nowadays, Jacques' kingdom was limited to a damp, bat infested cave, replete with dripping water, and the suffocating odor of mold and mildew which had worked its way into every scrap of clothing, drapery, and upholstery to be found. But things had not always been this way.

Until a little over three months ago a greater and more powerful Jacques had been the lord and master of a highly profitable and unchallenged gang of thieves and cutthroats, running rum, opium, guns, and occasionally a young woman or two though his vast network of black market dealers. The rum came from Jamaica, the opium from China, and the guns from Europe. The young women, who had been kidnapped for the white slave market, had come mainly from the brothels and dumps of the big eastern seaboard cities, but occasionally from the American frontier, where their abduction and disappearance would be blamed on the Indians.

His partner in crime, Jacob McPhearson, was the one behind the white slave trade, but Jacques had helped in providing transportation of the girls to eagerly awaiting men of means, both in the States, and worldwide. It was a risky business that brought great rewards.

But the whole thing had come down like a house of cards the day a man named Rue French had come into their lives. Jacques playacted the role of butler at the lavish office of Judge Bennet in Richmond, but did so for appearances only. Jacques, being a black man and former slave, could not be seen running the more legitimate side of his many business endeavors, most of which in turn supplied an easy and transparent means of disposing of the thousands of dollars which flowed through his coffers from his illegal dealings.

The Judge had been the perfect straw man, white, wealthy, politically connected, and an altogether stupid fellow, with no wit for business, and no talent for larceny. Within days following Rue French's visit, the Judge's house had been burned to the ground, and the Judge himself was found hanging by the neck in his own plush office, with any number of delicate papers and files gone missing. Worst of all, laying on the desk before the Judge's lifeless corpse was found a lengthy letter of admission, not only of his own guilty dealings, but of all known accomplices, and customers' homes, where stashes of contraband goods could be found, as well as the whereabouts of most of the young ladies who had been kidnapped and sold into slavery. Men had been hung, and shot, and fortunes and estates confiscated. The authorities were outraged and had acted swiftly and silently to smash the organization. Few stones had gone unturned. These doings would not find their way into the newspapers. Some things are best kept quiet.

And so now Jacques sat upon a throne of mildewed furniture taken from a contraband warehouse, as he and the handful of followers who remained with him ran hurriedly before the soldiers who had come for them back in Richmond. Their fate would be death if captured. This cave, often used in the past for the storage of stolen goods, was all that remained of Jacques' sordid empire. He spoke again to Layland.

"You come here to tell me this pack of lies! What do you hope to gain? Do you hope to swindle me? Look around you, fool, what is it that I have here that you dare to come and take from me? McPhearson's man French is the cause of all of this. He stole those girls, the gold, and somehow forced the Judge to write that letter of admission and the naming of our friends and benefactors."

"And now you try to tell me that this monster, Rue French, the very man that Jacob McPhearson has set upon us to destroy our operation, and take over the brotherhood for himself, is not who he says he is? Madness! I saw the man with my own eyes! I saw the letters and papers that McPhearson had written to destroy our organization. I was there!" Jacques was squirming in his chair as he spoke. His impatience had come to its limits. But he knew that he needed to regain his composure if he were to maintain control of his men. Layland answered softly.

"I have not come to anger you Jacques, and I have always been loyal to you. But it is my duty to tell you that the man you saw that day was not Rue French as you were led to believe. He was an impostor, using his disguise to free his daughter from the Judge's household. He had help, I am sure, but I do not know from where. It is possible that the Judge betrayed you as well. I do not know these things, but I do know that the man who truly is Rue French, the one whose name you have placed the death mark upon, was there at McPhearson's farm not three days ago, sitting on the front porch, and having a casual drink with the very man who had impersonated him. I know this man Rue French from my days up north, and I know the man who now holds claim to the farm which had once been in the hands of Jacob McPhearson. That man is none other than Brigadier General Henry James Stronton, and it was his daughter Ginny who he came to the Judge's office that day to recover. I heard them talking about it!"

Jacques sat quietly, his anger temporarily quelled by the words of his trusted servant. This would explain much. The papers which had been used to authenticate French's identity, the military precision of the attacks on the Judge's office, on his home, and on the farm held by McPhearson himself. Jacob had not been either seen or heard from for weeks before that day. Jacques considered the possibility that he had died in Stronton's raids, and that the entire organization rested now in his own skilled hands---alone. Rue French was the wild card that had yet to be dealt with. Jacques saw his opportunity for greatness once again.

"Was there anything else of value that you saw or heard while you were listening to their words, Layland?" Putting this man at ease could yield information that might not have seemed so very important at the first telling, but might prove to be the key to success in the final analysis. Jacques was very proud of his ability to think beyond the obvious, and to gain leverage over weaker men.

"There is maybe one thing---Rue French, the real Rue French, was talking to his horse out in the stables as he left early yesterday morning, before the others had awakened. He told his horse that he was planning to wipe out the poison that General Stronton had failed to destroy. I believe by that he meant he is coming for you, my friend. He intends to kill us all. But with the way he left, in secret, I believe there now to be bad blood between him and the General, possibly over the girl."

Jacques realized now that putting a death mark on a man as vicious as Rue French might have been an unwise move on his part. Nevertheless, a division between the General and French could be turned to his advantage given the right cir cumstances. The girl could be of great value now---as bait.

"Your words are of great importance, Layland, my old friend. I will ponder these things tonight, and devise a plan which will help us to rebuild our empire." Jacques dismissed the kneeling Layland with a flick of his wrist, and the faithful servant hurriedly stepped away from the presence of the moody and unpredictable Jacques, before he changed his mind. Even loyalty knew the need to for discretion from time to time.

Jacques stepped away from his throne and put the matter to much thought. There was an opportunity here to be sure. It would most certainly be a chance for greatness once again, but perhaps at the risk of a painful death. The bounty had not been successful, and many of their best men had apparently died trying. The truth of the matter became clearly evident to the scheming Jacques. A temporary alliance with this man from the north could buy time. But dealing with a man such as that was dangerous at best. There could only be one man in charge here.

In order for him to stay alive, Rue French must die.

# CHAPTER NINETEEN

The wooden swing hung from sturdy ropes nearly twenty feet in length, the giant spreading oak tree unchallenged by the weight of the woman-child who glided to and
fro in the early autumn sun. Ginny Stronton looked for all
the world like she hadn't a care in the world, playfully enjoying this moment of peace and contentment. Nothing could
have been further from the truth.

It had been three days now since John Cummins, the man
she loved, had ridden away, unannounced, in the early pre-
dawn hours. He had made no mention of his leaving, no
hint to warn her. She awoke that morning to find that he was
simply not there, leaving no trace of his passing.

And now there was a divide between her and her father,
her hero, the man who had been faithful in the time of her
greatest need. His disapproval of John went much deeper
than simply regarding the man as an unworthy suitor. Ginny

could hear and see a hardness in her father that had not been there before. The words between them these last few days had brought tears and anger, until now there were very few words between them at all.

Ginny was once again alone in the midst of people. The farm was flourishing with activity, with the crops coming in, and the preparations for the long winter months ahead. Color was finding its way into the trees in the nearby hills. The beauty was as undeniable as her sadness. She had to do something.

Henry Stronton knew that his latest rage over John Cummins had gone too far, and that his precious daughter was hurting, not only from his harsh words, but from the loss of the man she had fallen in love with. Stronton was a father, and therefore a man, and as guilty as most of his species of not understanding the womenfolk in his life. But he knew what he felt---he loved his daughter, and would lay down his life for her. He also knew that he did not trust John Cummins, and that he wanted that man dead to protect Ginny.

The longer he put this off, the deeper the chasm between them would become. A man never benefited from arguing with a woman, especially one from his own family. This constant conflict was tearing them apart. He had this thing to do, so he'd best be on with it.

Stronton spent the rest of that day making preparations for his departure, packing what was needed, and speaking with some of his most trusted men concerning his plans, and their need to watch over his daughter. Henry Stronton was a man of details.

He worked hard at being genial and happy at dinner that night, giving no hint of his intentions, or of the mission ahead of him---to remove Rue French's presence from this earth, and hopefully save his daughter's life.

In the pre-dawn hours of the following morning, Stronton walked quietly down the steps to the stables, and mounting up, rode for Richmond, and his rendezvous with John Cummins, aka Rue French.

He did not stop to say goodbye.

That morning was not a happy time there at Dellmont. Ginny Stronton's rage coursed heatedly through her veins this day as she ran her horse farther and faster than ever before. The two men she loved so dearly, those two wonderful, stubborn, pig-headed men had both snuck out on her before dawn on two separate days, avoiding her like school boys hiding from their teacher. Twice! The outrage!

She knew what this was all about. It hadn't taken her long to sort things out. One ran off to be the chivalrous knight of old, slaying her dragons and upholding her honor, while the other one, the king of the realm, went off to slay the knight, himself wanting to be the one who slayed her dragons, heedless and uncaring of what the girl herself wanted in the first place. Men!

Having gotten both herself and the horse up into a lather, Ginny Stronton, the General's daughter, took charge of the situation and started handing out some orders of her own. Men were called to action and plans were put into place.

She then ran to her newly built bedroom to quickly change and pack a bag. The carriage had been made ready in minutes, and men at arms would ride this day by her side. Her lot was cast. She would bring back these two valiant warriors, each of whom had each gone off to fight a vain battle for her sake. She would then put these two childlike men in their place and have peace between them once and for all. Enough was enough! The lady of the castle had spoken.

Then, as she picked up the reins to leave, she whispered a little prayer for her journey, and for the two men that she loved.

The men that she loved---Ginny smiled at the realization. The whip cracked. Her race against fate had begun.

The mask of Rue French hung heavily over the countenance of John Cummins, so much so that the man that Ginny Stronton had come to know, the man over whom she now was investing so much worry and frustration, had once again nearly ceased to exist.

If men are indeed their own worst enemies, then John Cummins' foe would be a power greater than himself, greater than his skills, and far more deadly to himself than any other man alive. For he was riding not only against the mirage of those who would harm his beloved Ginny, but also against the paradox of the man whose reputation preceded him---Rue French.

This was a name of legend, a boogie man of sorts, mostly made up in the minds of those who love a good lie. Rue French was a name he had been given, and not one that he had ever used himself. He was credited with murders he had never committed, robberies he had never attempted, and a type of brutal nastiness he had never been a part of.

John Cummins was sneaky, yes, and quick with a gun, but only when necessary. He had killed, or he would have been killed. He had robbed, but always and only from those who routinely robbed others. He had pretended to be men other than himself, with skills and privileges he had never earned, and always at the expense of those who had tried to profit from associating with a man as worthy and important as the men he had pretended to be.

The irony of this moment was not lost on him. A death mark, a bounty of $10,000, had been placed on the head of Rue French. And all because a man looking for his lost daughter had gone and pretended to be Rue French, a character who made his living impersonating others. Sooner or later a man is forced to pay the piper for his fun. But things seemed different now.

Ginny Stronton was the difference. She was pretty, and full of wonder and grit. She had somehow opened the door back to the man he had once been, providing a way for him to move once again out into the sunlight and to walk away from the inescapable prison he had built with his own hands---that being his living shrine to the betrayer of his soul---Priscilla.

Such a fool he had become, living his wanton life for the sake of a woman who never loved him, a woman who had used him as her toy. He had been ambitious, and careless, desiring Priscilla for her unequaled beauty, ignoring those around him who had dared to tell him the simple truth---she was no good.

But this girl, Ginny, had shown him the truth, and forged a bond between them which must never be broken. There were those who could still threaten her, and her happiness. John Cummins would find them and destroy them. And if Rue French were to take the blame, fine. He would put on the mask of Rue French to complete this task, and then set it aside forever, returning to Ginny with the words of assurance he knew in his heart that she needed to hear---that her past was now dead to the world, and she could live free from fear once again.

But first things first. He needed information, and he needed help. He would find both at the home of a well-known courtesan, here on the outskirts of Richmond. He straightened his tie and brushed off his coat. This was a business meeting, and gold would change hands this day. John Cummins would never have visited such a house of ill repute for pleasure. But Rue French knew the darker side of society well, and how to profit by working with those who excelled at their trade. A simple knock, and a knowing smile was all that was needed here. The plan was set in motion.

# CHAPTER TWENTY

O nce again Brigadier General Stronton had found welcome in the home of Ben Chalmers, lifelong friend,
and comrade in the many years of struggle serving with the
Army of Virginia. Stronton had always been an honored guest
in this home, a guest who would never need an invitation to
stay the night. This was a bond as deep as the sea.

Only months before, Stronton had sat at this very spot,
holding the hand of his cherished daughter, Ginny, who he
had only hours earlier rescued from the lecherous grasp of
one Judge Bennet, known to be the right hand man of the
hated Jacob McPhearson. But the evil in Richmond seemed
to have survived the scourge that Stronton and his men
had visited upon that den of thieves, indicated by the death
mark which had been placed upon Rue French, the man the
General had impersonated, the very man that had slept under
his roof only days before. The General was troubled.

"Ben, I'm in a fix. I'm here today on my way to Richmond to settle scores with the man known as Rue French. That's the man I impersonated to get Ginny back. The thing is, there really is a Rue French, and he rode right up to our door just a few days ago, thinking he would find someone else there- -that being Jacob McPhearson, the man I tracked halfway across the country, only to find him laying in an unmarked grave out in the middle of the Kansas prairie. Jacob had been hunting his niece, Catherine O'Dell, the same girl that deeded Dellmont over to me and Ginny, and who gave me the background I needed to dress up like French."

Ben's head was spinning. He had only heard bits and pieces of this story up until now, and hearing all of this was too much to swallow in one gulp.

"Let me get this straight, General. You rode all over everywhere looking for the man who you thought had Ginny, while he was riding all over everywhere looking for this Catherine O'Dell person, but you found him dead, and Catherine O'Dell gave you her farm---is that about it?" Ben didn't smell any liquor on Stronton, but he did think that this tale was a bit far-fetched.

"I can't prove it Ben, but it's true. And I have to believe there's a lot more to that story that I'll never know. I tell you, just sitting and talking to that O'Dell girl gave me the willies. It was almost like she had some sort of mystical power about her or something. Her eyes seemed to see everything at once. She was quite a lady. And she'd been Ginny's friend for a short time, right there on the farm.

"So what takes you to Richmond? Seems to me you're pretty well set up there where you are. And you seem to have made out alright with this French fellow." The General sat there quietly for a few moments, choosing his words.

"This Rue French fellow is a killer, and a thief. He's as smooth as molasses, and it seems he swept Ginny right off her feet in just the matter of a few days. Knowing the kind of man he is, and after all that Ginny has been through, I figured to run him off the place. But then one morning he gets up and rides out before dawn without so much as a "by your leave" on the way out. Ginny hasn't been the same since, and I'm on my way to Richmond to locate this man and kill him. I won't let him ruin Ginny's life again the way he and others like him did before." Ben had listened carefully, and seeing the fire and frustration in his old comrade's eyes, knew that there was something else at play here, something as of yet unsaid.

"But you're not sure of yourself, are you old friend? You've always told me not to live in the past, or you'll ruin all your tomorrows. I don't know this French fellow, but I do know Ginny, and I knew her mother, and they're a lot alike. If I remember right, there was a little tarnish on your armor when Ruthie set her cap to marry you. Murder is a serious business, Henry. Are you intending to kill this man for making Ginny happy two days ago, or because he knew someone who had made her unhappy a year ago? Be careful how you answer this—something isn't right in your thinking." Ben watched as the General sipped his coffee, now growing cold from disuse. The man was worn out, and all this confusion had taken a toll on his features. Henry Stronton was a worried man.

"You always could read me like a book, Lieutenant. It doesn't do a man good to go into battle without a clear plan, or without a total resolve concerning his enemy. What if I am wrong? Maybe I should be going after this man to hog tie him and drag him back to my daughter—I haven't seen her so happy in years as she was while he was there. They seemed to have a kinship of some sorts, something I don't think I understand, but it was there, I saw it, and I hated it."

"You said he stayed with you for several days. Was he holding you at gun point? How is it he stayed for so long if you didn't want him there?"

"As a matter of fact, it was at gun point---but it was my gun that was being trained on him come to think of it. I was prepared to shoot him down on the spot when he first arrived, but Ginny talked sense, saying that we should at least give the man a chance to say his piece before we shot him dead. And you're right, she is a lot like her mother."

"And so you held the man that you're intending to kill at gun point for several days without killing him, while he sweeps your daughter off her feet while you're watching, and then you waited a week to decide to go out after him and to kill him because he made your daughter happy? I think maybe I need to switch out that coffee for something a little stronger. You need to get a good night's sleep my friend. You're making no sense at all. What did you say this man's name was?"

"Rue French, but his real name is John Cummins, and now that I think about it, he seemed to be a pretty good fellow."

There's nothing like talking with a true friend to help you see the truth behind your troubles---because it's usually yourself.

Major Winston Benedict had graduated in the lower half of his academy's class, had no record of distinguished action with which to enthrall the press, and was not particularly good looking. But he did have one thing about him that made him not only popular, but in high demand among those with a certain level of discretion---he was rich.

Very rich in fact. Money had gotten him the most comfortable of assignments, the best quarters, and some of the best-tailored uniforms to be found among the many officers in the Union Army. It was his misfortune to have been wearing his splendid garb as he entered the home of one Eliza Standish, better known in her circles as "Electra". She was a seasoned professional, skilled at her trade, which itself went by many names. Most folks simply referred to her work as "the oldest profession", and left it at that.

Eliza was exceedingly beautiful, and except for a few difficult times toward the end of the war, had found her business steady and lucrative, what with so many lonely men so far from home. She was a very good listener, and the sound of coins, one upon the other, was the best way to get her attention.

Rue French had an abundance of coin, but no appetite for a woman such as Electra, except for her cunning, her skill, and her willingness to do almost anything for money. The young and inexperienced Major Benedict would be no match for the lady's charms, but even less so for the drugged wine of which he so eagerly drank. Within minutes the sleeping Benedict was whisked through a dark door, wearing only his Union suit. He was laid carefully into the back of a waiting wagon, placed there among crates carrying chickens, traveling to a far-away town. He would be discovered the next morning, suffering from a terrible headache, and lying in a pile of horse manure out behind a barn. Major Winston Benedict would have much explaining to do, and a very difficult time getting back to his barracks in Richmond.

Meanwhile, the Major's finely tailored uniform, complete with his equally magnificent horse, rode confidently toward the hills outside of Lynchburg, and on toward the stronghold of Jacques Benine, a name and a location obtained at gunpoint by a man whose legend was equal to his skills --- Rue French. The man of many disguises would now not only have the splendid uniform of a high ranking officer to wear, but also the soldiers of the Union army to assist him in his quest.

His plan was working seamlessly.

# CHAPTER TWENTY-ONE

G inny Stronton could be forgiven for not planning this trip all that carefully. Her sudden decision to hop in a carriage and retrieve the men she loved was the result of a heated discussion she was having with herself, and no outside influence was there to dissuade her--not that it could have.

John Cummins had gone off on a tangent to finish the job her father had begun months before---to rid Virginia of the vermin which had grown fat and comfortable under the protective cloak of Jacob McPhearson. Jacob's death, along with the death of Judge Bennet and his followers had not been enough. He was certain that a spark still remained of that hellish fire, and he had gone to stamp it out once and for all.

This had all been decided in a characteristic moment of bravado, and Cummins was not to be deterred. That was why he had left before dawn that day. But an equally inspired moment had found her father sneaking off before dawn just a few days later, apparently to deal with the absent Cummins. She was absolutely certain that both men had taken up their quests on her behalf, and had snuck off as they did knowing full well that she wouldn't have allowed it. It had fallen now to her to bring these two back home where they belonged so that they could all three get on with their lives. Ginny's father was English, and she was like him in the ways of strategies and planning. But her mother was of Irish stock, and at this moment any thoughts of planning had been set aside, while her Irish temper ruled the day. The carriage was urged on a little faster. Ginny's impatience grew as the miles went on and on. Evening was falling while she and her retainers were still many miles from Richmond, the town she was certain that both her father and John Cummins had ridden to days before.

Ginny was not traveling alone. Before he left, Stronton had assigned two men, Milo Heslin, and Xander Riverton, to stay by Ginny's side day and night, as protectors and defenders. Both men had served with the General during the war, and now worked on the newly blossoming Dellmont estate, as trusted as family, and as loyal.

Milo was a quiet fellow of average height with arms like tree trunks. Whatever he picked up got lifted, and whatever he pushed got moved. Xander's real name was Alexander, but he didn't care much for the name---so Xander it was. And no man would be fool enough to argue the point. He was a very large man, who always rode a very large horse. These two would serve as Ginny's bodyguards on this trip. Wherever she went, they had to follow.

They rode up to an inn with rooms to let. It was a place of good reputation, and as the hour was getting late, they wisely pulled off the road to stay the night.

The innkeeper was a kindly fellow, and offered Ginny a clean room downstairs, near to where he and his wife would be sleeping. The two men would have to sleep in the dining hall near the fire as no other rooms were available. Traffic on this main road had increased once again now that Richmond was in the midst of rebuilding, and the opportunities for sales and investments loomed large. The inn had once again become a busy place.

The innkeeper's wife served up a fine meal of rabbit stew and fresh baked bread with honey, followed up by a raspberry cobbler. It was delicious. The other boarders came and ate as well, all of the men quite courteous and thoughtful in the presence of such a lovely young lady. Ginny stayed near the fire and enjoyed the conversation of a pair of actors, traveling to the coast for what promised to be a month-long stay with a recently formed Shakespeare company. They were excited about the return of classical theater, and expertly quoted verse after verse of poetry to the appreciative audience which had gathered around.

Of course, there is always the opportunity for a fool to be a fool. And sure enough, while Milo and Xander were out seeing to the horses for the night, a rather imposing man of middle age decided that the young lady needed to leave the company of those whom he considered to be "girlish" actors, and spend her evening seeing to his carnal desires instead. Ginny refused and one of the salesmen stepped in to remove the man's grip from the girl's arm.

Dark and formidable, Ginny's assailant used his free hand to swat the man aside, sending him sprawling across the room and into a table. He then reached down with that same hand, and pulling his pistol, threatened a deadlier response to anyone else who would dare interfere. He began to drag the struggling Ginny toward the stairs.

He never got there. In fact, he didn't even manage another step, as he suddenly found himself lifted high above the floor, and being carried toward the door like an old piece of furniture. At that same moment a hot brand from the fire was placed on his wrist, causing him to drop the pistol with a scream of pain. He released his grip on Ginny's arm as well, and started bellowing his displeasure of this turn of events. His language was quite colorful. Milo held the door as Xander continued to carry the unhappy bully none too gently out to the livery barn, with no one willing to stand in their way.

The astonished and fearful faces of the other travelers were calmed as Ginny explained to them all that these two men had been assigned by her father to protect her on her journey, and that she knew that she had never been in any real danger. Relieved laughter ensued as the crowd told and retold the events of the last few moments, and the evening continued in story and song as though nothing had ever happened. Even the salesman who had tried to intervene seemed none the worse for wear, and was enjoying a stein of grog "on the house" for his efforts.

It was dark by the time Milo and Xander came back in through the door, with no sign of the fellow that had been carried out. Milo explained.

"That fellow will not be coming back in tonight, and apologizes for his rudeness toward the young lady, the gentleman he struck, and to all of you who might have felt threatened by his actions. He is sincerely sorry for his rudeness, and I assure you that he won't be bothering you anymore this evening. As it is, he has decided to stay the night in the barn, away from all of you good people, in order to hide his shame for his very rude behavior, and to reflect on his sins." Then it was Xander who had the last word on the matter.

"In fact, he was so sorry for his rudeness, he agreed for Milo and me to use his room tonight, and he'll even foot the bill for our meals as well." Xander laid down a gold piece in front of the innkeeper, more than enough to cover the debt. It was a gold piece which had until recently been housed in the ruffian's pocket.

That unfortunate fellow would not be spending that coin this night, as he instead found himself hanging hand and foot from an overhead beam in the horse barn, a good twenty feet above the stalls below. The pain from his bruised and battered body would remind him of his indiscretion towards the lady, and the bait of corn his wardens had left in his shirt would surely interest the local night life, be they birds, possums, raccoons, or rats.

That was Milo's idea. He said he didn't want the fellow to be alone and scared of the dark. It was Xander's idea to tie his mouth shut, so he wouldn't be waking anyone up during the night with his yelling and crying and screaming and such. They would check on him in the morning.

He was lucky they had let him live.

The travelers from Dellmont got off to an early start that next morning, with Ginny already in a froth to get going. But it wasn't long until things had changed, another matter standing front and center.

The carriage now sat still by the side of the road---the horse was willing, but the driver was not. Ginny Stronton had pulled up just as they had arrived at the outskirts of Richmond. She could go no further, overwhelmed by memories, paralyzed by the fear of what could be.

She had come to find the men she loved, but an invisible barrier now stood in her way. She had not been back to Richmond since that day that her father had rescued her from Judge Bennet's snare. Memories clouded her purpose, and fear gripped her body. Her bodyguards were also her friends, having known her since back when she was just a young girl. They needed to intervene here, and now.

"Pardon my saying so, Miss Stronton, but I doubt that we will be finding your father riding out here on this road, heading our way on that big horse of his. If he's here, he'll more than likely be in town, and that's straight ahead." Both men were still sitting on their horses, looking down at this cherished young woman, who had become frozen in fear, but still able to gather the courage to speak the truth.

"I'm afraid, Milo. I'm afraid someone's going to recognize me, and point at me and laugh. I thought I was alright now back at the farm, but this is different. I'm scared to be around people. They'll laugh at me, and they'll laugh at Daddy." Her shame for herself was her shame for her father as well. What kind of man had a concubine for a daughter? Maybe she'd be better off dead. Milo spoke again.

"I will personally thrash any man who says anything against you anyplace, anytime. And I would enjoy the doing of it. But you need to understand, and hear me out now, there is a big difference between what people force you to do and what you do on your own. We all know what happened, and I assure you that the Judge who put you in that position died a horrible death--a coward's death. You are a lovely young woman, and the daughter of one of the finest men I have ever known. We are not going to force you to go into Richmond. You will go ahead by your own will because of the love you have for your father, and for that man John Cummins. They need you, and it is right that you are here. But I wish you'd hurry up and get on with it, 'cause I'm tired of sitting on this horse, and I think it's getting tired of me sitting on it as well." A smile came to Ginny's face then, and soon a good hearty laugh. The spell was broken. A quick click of the reins and the carriage continued on. Ginny was talkative again.

"By the way, whatever happened to that fellow you two carried out of the tavern last night? I don't believe I saw him anywhere around this morning. And how in the world did you manage to pick up a man that large and carry him out the door like so much laundry?" Ginny knew full well that these two men were quite capable of handling anything they put their minds to. She only hoped they hadn't gone too far. Xander told the tale.

"Well, Miss Ginny, it's like this. That man was full of meanness, and meanness can look mighty big and bad when it's beating up on someone smaller, or it's threatening you with a weapon or some such. But the fact is, meanness is pretty light weight stuff, and a man full of meanness has no strength in him at all, in fact, he's all hollow and empty inside. Carrying him out the door was no more a problem than carrying an empty barrel." Milo shared a few more details.

"Xander's right ma'am, he wasn't much. We kept him tied up in the barn overnight and went out and sent him on his way this morning. He did have a few scratch marks on him where it seemed he'd been arguing with a raccoon about some corn, but all and all I think we were very gentle in the way we dealt with his ill-mannered ways." The two men smiled at one another then, and Ginny knew there was far more to the story than she'd probably ever know. Right at that moment she figured she was the safest girl in town. And she was.

Just a little bit further and they ran smack dab into Richmond, or at least the hustle and bustle that was Richmond these days. People were everywhere, and likewise were the sounds of hammers and saws and voices being raised. The spirit of renewal was quickly replacing the burned out visage of a town in ashes.

"How are we going to find Daddy in all of this? There are people everywhere! I wouldn't even know where to begin." She was right. This was a giant puzzle without any clues. Even a man who stood out in a crowd as much as the General would be hard to find in this herd of humanity. They needed a plan.

"Milo, you stay with Ginny, and ride through the main streets. I'll split off and check the stables and such and see if anyone has seen him. This town isn't big enough for anyone to hide in for long. We'll meet up again right here in two hours' time." None of them were carrying a time piece, and no clock could be seen on any remaining church tower. They'd just have to guess at the two hours.

Xander rode off to a nearby stable while Ginny and Milo worked their way down the busy streets. There was no sign of the General or of his horse. Nor was there any sign of John Cummins. Ginny would know John's horse on sight. Even more importantly, there was no sign of any of the men Ginny had met while captive at the Judge's home. It seemed her fears were for naught.

# CHAPTER TWENTY-TWO

L ife holds many mysteries, and the intertwining of people's
lives, one with another, is a continual matter for wonder and
amazement for all of mankind. How often folks had been searching for a certain something, or someone, and found a treasure
quite different than the one they had been looking for, a surprise and a blessing just waiting for them to come and discover.
And so it was, that while Ginny had worked herself up to a lather
to find Henry Stronton and John Cummins, and to bring them
back home with her, she found instead a part of herself, Heaven's
very different plan for her journey to Richmond that day.

Ginny had been carefully searching, scanning the sea of
faces in a desperate effort to see without being seen. But the
one person who needed to be found was suddenly right there
before her eyes, and only a few feet away. Leaning against the
side of a building in the noonday autumn sun stood a memory
of those terrible days. There was no mistaking her.

Ginny stopped the carriage and hurriedly got down, running the few steps needed to cover the distance to the ragged figure, thin and gaunt. She looked her long-lost memory in the eyes, hoping for some sign of recognition. It came, slowly, cautiously, and then climaxed in the embrace of reunion that only tormented souls could understand.

"Ginny?"

This young blond-haired girl, ragged and worn, was none other than Francine, Ginny's former roommate and fellow captive at the Judge's home. She had been rescued along with two other girls when the house had been raided by the General's men, using information that Ginny herself had supplied. Ginny had understood that all those girls had been reunited with their families and were happily back home again, just as she was. Something had gone terribly wrong.

"When was the last time you ate?" There was no reason for niceties here, no catching up that needed to be done. Francine's condition was apparent. Milo came over and helped Francine into the carriage. There was a cafe that they had passed just a few doors down. This girl needed a meal, and clean clothes, and someone to care for her. She would find all that she needed this day, and more.

Milo draped his coat around Francine's shoulders as he helped her in to find a seat, while Ginny went up to the proprietor to ask for some warm broth, and to arrange for any fresh vegetables and fruits that might be available. A coin had already passed hands before she returned to the table. That coin would be more than enough to pay for a dozen meals. No questions would be asked.

Milo held the girl close to him, his big strong arms as reassuring as a lullaby. His usually witty humor had changed to a litany of comfort that Francine did not resist. The food was served quickly and discreetly, with the other guests now having no reason to take notice. Francine wept as she ate, often pausing to wipe her eyes on the soft white handkerchief Ginny had provided. The kinship here between these two women was woven in those countless hours of fear and anguish, ripped apart from those they loved and forced to serve in a life of bondage and shame.

But for all of that, it was a slice of apple pie that brought the smiles back to Francine's face, once again glowing and alive, just as Ginny had remembered her. The reunion was complete. And Ginny quickly took charge.

"Where do you live?" Ginny had no intention of letting her friend go back to the street where she had found her, but was concerned that Francine's entire family might have fallen on hard times like this.

"I live where you found me. I sleep where I can. My folks wouldn't take me back. They said I was damaged goods, and no longer their daughter. They turned me out. I came back here to Richmond to try to find work. But there is no work here for a woman, except in the shacks behind the railroad. And I won't do that---never again. I'll die first. I even tried begging but it wasn't enough. Even the church turned me away. Ginny, how did you ever find me? Who sent you here?" Milo and Ginny exchanged glances. That would be a question that they might never know the answer to, no matter how they puzzled it out. They came looking for two men, and had found this girl instead. They both knew that from this point on, Francine would be a welcomed part of their lives, like family. It didn't even need to be discussed. Francine had come home at last.

"We'll talk about that later. Right now, we need to get you into some clean clothes. As you remember, nothing I wear would ever be big enough to fit you. We need to find something in your size." While Ginny was more the thin and limber type, Francine leaned much more toward the classic hour glass shape, and even when they were roommates, they never mistook one girl's clothes for the other's.

Before they had made their last turn in search of the General, Ginny had spotted a millinery shop, with several sensible-looking dresses displayed in the window. This would be as good a place as any to start. The door was open and Ginny sent Francine on in to get things started while she made arrangements for Milo to meet up with Xander as the two hours were already almost up. Then, just as Ginny turned to go in, she saw Francine run back out in tears, collapsing onto the ground below, cringing in bitter defeat.

"What happened? What's wrong?" Milo stood watch as Ginny knelt down to comfort her friend. Something awful had just happened, and the General's daughter was determined to know why.

"She called me dirty. She said she wouldn't wait on a tramp like me. She called me a street walker, and trash! She pushed me out through the door."

This moment would be the turning point in young Ginny Stronton's life. The very degradation and slurs that she had feared for herself had just been showered upon her friend, and fellow captor. Shame and disgrace were now replaced by righteous anger and venom. It had gone far enough. She would hide no more. It all stopped here and now.

"Milo, give me your gun. You stay here with Francine no matter what. What needs to happen in there is mine to do. Do you understand?" Milo handed over the weapon, his face stoic but his eyes smiling. This was General Stronton's daughter alright. The one he remembered when she was just a young girl, with the grit and spirit of her mother, God rest her soul. Whatever was going to take place in that dress shop, he would not be needed. Little Ginny was back.

Ginny went through the door with her head filled with a tempered rage that took all of the air out of the room. She walked directly up to the woman standing behind a table filled with hats, grabbed a handful of the woman's dress and slammed her against the nearby wall in a most unladylike manner. The gun then came up and found a comfortable resting place right under the woman's chin. The suddenness and ferociousness of Ginny's attack held her motionless.

"Listen to me very carefully. I am Virginia Gail Stronton, daughter of Brigadier General Henry James Stronton, formerly commander of the armies of the Commonwealth of Virginia. The young woman who you just threw out of your establishment is my best friend, whom I have personally rescued from the gates of hell this very day."

"Whatever she is, or has been, so have I been as well. I see by the look on your face that I have your attention. You will now pay equal attention to my good friend, just as you now do me. I will lay three gold pieces on that table over there. That will be more than enough to cover any items that she may choose. Do you agree to my terms?" The woman made a vain effort to nod, the pistol's barrel pushing much too hard against her chin to allow any motion. A guttural reply was the best she could do. Ginny smiled then, and leaning forward planted a gentle kiss on the surprised woman's forehead, gently releasing her from her grip.

"The kiss was for your forgiveness, for I might have been a little forward just now. But it will also serve as a reminder---if you or anyone working with you here so much as looks sideways at my dear friend again, I will send a bullet from this pistol right to the spot I marked with my lips. Try to remember." With that, Ginny poked the woman's forehead with her finger, and smiled. She turned to bring Francine in from the street, and heard a loud thud behind her.

The terrified woman had fainted dead away.

# CHAPTER TWENTY-THREE

L ieutenant Robert Tresser would have made Captain by
now if the war hadn't ended when it did.  Sharp, strong,
and respected by his men, Tresser was the kind of commander
that could win a war.  The United States army was lucky to
have him, and many more like him.

For most folks, the war between the States had ended.  But
here and there across the country, from the Atlantic seaboard
to Texas and back, small bands of organized resistance main-
tained the fight, often in guerrilla outfits that used hit and
run tactics to harass the Yankee troops stationed throughout
the South.  Oft times these so called "patriots" were actually
little more than bandits, hiding behind the Stars and Bars to
gain sympathy for their rampage of robbing and killing.

It was groups such as these that Lieutenant Tresser and
his men were assigned to locate and eliminate as a threat,
and to do so by whatever means necessary.  Tresser's outfit

was deployed over by the foothills of the Smoky Mountains, a hotbed of rebel sympathy, and an ideal place to hide.

Tresser's troops had set up camp near an abandoned farmhouse, and were obliged to live off the land as the need would arise. He had twenty men in his command, living in tents whenever there was enough time to put them up, and worn out from their nonstop pursuit of an invisible enemy.

The Lieutenant was enjoying the cool early autumn air, along with a warm campfire, when up out of nowhere came a rider on horseback, wearing an officer's uniform and riding a fine mount. Dressed as well as the man looked to be, Tresser knew that this fellow was most likely his superior, and whatever devilment he brought with him would require the Lieutenant to be in proper uniform and ready for inspection. He went to his tent, and gathering up his hat and sword, strolled out to meet his visitor.

The officer had already made his way past the sentry, and still mounted, rode right up to the fire. When he spoke, an air of competent authority filled the air.

"Good afternoon. My name is Crittendon, and I require to speak to the officer in charge of this unit. Who would that be, Lieutenant?" He look straight into Tresser's eyes, but with an air of respect that Tresser was not used to experiencing when dealing with officers of superior rank. There was something decidedly different about this man.

"Good afternoon, Major, and welcome. I'm Lieutenant Robert Tresser, and this unit is under my command. How may I be of service, sir?" It was certain that this officer hadn't ridden all the way out there on a whim. Whatever he wanted was best gotten on with as soon as possible. Tresser had work to do.

"Lieutenant, I carry written orders to spearhead an effort to rid this area of a known smuggler and thief by the name of Jacques Benine and the gang of cutthroats that he runs with. I have become privy to special intelligence that will aid in this effort. That explains my presence here. I wish to assure you, sir, that while I do hold superior rank, and am in charge of this operation, I intend that you will maintain direct command over the men in your company as would be your regular practice. Your record speaks for itself Lieutenant, and I would be unworthy of this uniform if I were to take direct command of these men from an officer that is as respected and trusted as yourself. Are you in agreement to this arrangement, Lieutenant?" Tresser was heartened by this officer's direct and no-nonsense approach. Looking at the Major's uniform, so carefully tailored and fitted, he had figured the man would be nothing more than some air-headed poppinjay, far more likely to get men killed than led to victory. He was pleasantly surprised.

"Yes, sir, and I thank you, sir. It will be an honor to serve with you, sir. If it pleases the Major, Private Hottle here will care for your mount, while you have a chance to rest up before dinner. It's groundhog tonight sir, excellent in a stew. I will of course be happy to move out of my tent to make room for you during your stay. Is there anything else we can do to make you comfortable, sir?" The Lieutenant hated giving up his tent, and now would be forced to sleep in the Sergeant's tent, along with that man's fearsome snoring. The Major would have nothing to do with it.

"I'll thank you to stay in your own tent, Lieutenant, and I'll simply bunk up with you. I have my own bedroll here, along with a few odds and ends. This is no pleasure trip for me, any more than it is for you. In addition, since you know the terrain around these parts far better than I do, I'll be relying on your judgment in helping me to finalize our plans. Chasing you down in another tent when I get some hair-brained idea is simply out of the question. Besides, I wasn't always a Major, you know." Crittendon dismounted, and taking his bedroll, followed Tresser to the command tent. Private Hottle marveled at the lines on the magnificent horse as he led it off for grooming. It must run fast as greased lightning!

And so it was that John Cummins had gained the armed might of a detachment of United States cavalry, willing to do his bidding under falsified orders, to deal with the evil which was Jacques Benine, known to many only as Judge Bennet's butler. It was this Jacques who had ordered Rue French dead, and put that enormous price on his head. This was a score that would be settled, and very soon.

It required the help of the dress maker, who had remained hidden in the back of the millinery shop, to revive the fainted form of her sister, the one with whom Ginny had spoken to, using Milo's pistol for emphasis. Not so genuine apologies were made all around, mostly so that all parties could save face and get on with the business at hand. The gold coins still sitting on the hat table did much to change the quality of the air in the room, allowing the clerk to breathe far more freely than before. Gold can have a soothing effect on some folks.

For the sake of propriety, it was agreed that Ginny would take a stroll up and down the many shops which were scattered around the area, supposedly looking for John Cummins, while

Francine stayed behind for her fitting, with Milo close by to offer his opinion as needed. It was apparent that Francine really liked the idea of having this powerful man nearby, and thoroughly enjoyed modeling garment after garment for his appraisal.

At first Ginny was not all that sold on this arrangement, but she knew that Francine was in good hands with Milo there, and that she herself had maybe gone a little too far in the righteous anger she had plied upon the terrified seamstress. Then again it could just have easily been her standing there by the streets in rags had it not been for the unfailing love and courage of her father.

Her father! She had nearly forgotten about the reason they had come to Richmond in the first place. And worse, in her efforts to help her dear friend Francine, she had failed to send Milo back to the rendezvous where Xander was no doubt impatiently waiting for them. It was obvious that her father's gift of strategy had been lost on her. She marched back toward the dress shop in a hurry.

"Milo, we have a problem!" The force of her voice could be heard halfway down the block, and all eyes turned to see what all the commotion was about. Ginny walked through the door only to find three people huddled around the newly fallen form of the seamstress, who once again had fainted, reacting in abject terror to what she feared was the returning wrath of the woman with the pistol.

It seemed Ginny was far more ready for her return to society, than society was for her to be back.

The rest of the day proved to be much too uneventful. Francine was able to put together a sensible wardrobe, and Milo finally did get back in touch with Xander.

But there was no sign of the General. Two men mentioned that they had seen a fellow who met the description the morning before, but nothing since. Money was left in the hands of people who knew how to see everything, and as the afternoon drew on, it was apparent to Ginny that they had come up empty handed. It just didn't make sense.

As a group, a newly formed foursome with Francine now included, it was decided that it was not in their best interests to stay the night in Richmond. Accommodations were few and far between, and it wasn't all that far back to the little tavern where they had stayed the night before. Even as much as Ginny hated leaving Richmond without having found John or her father, common sense won out over stubbornness.

As the carriage with its two powerful escorts headed westward, and back out of town, a nearby window's curtain fell back into place, once again shielding the man holding the knife, as well as his captive, bound and gagged, but not much the worse for wear. Not yet.

"You see, General, just as I promised. Your little girl and her friends have been allowed to leave without harm, and none the wiser. The day will come when she will learn of your death, at the hands of blood thirsty cutthroats no doubt. But no harm will come to her, just as I have promised. You, however, will suffer the anguish of hell before I am finished with you. You see, there is a man that I intend to introduce to you on my terms, a fellow not known for his generosity in these matters."

"You somehow managed to impersonate one of the most feared and dangerous men in America, and in doing so put an undeserved death mark on his head. I will truly enjoy watching you suffer at the hands of the real Rue French. He obviously spared you out of some mislaid courtesy on his part. I simply assume that he has no idea as to your role in his recent troubles. You met him once and survived. Your next meeting will prove very different."

Jacques' smile couldn't hide his pure meanness. He was enjoying this. Being lord and master over a Confederate General made him a much bigger man. He was going to make the most of it.

# CHAPTER TWENTY-FOUR

Lieutenant Tresser had been with his new C.O. only four days now, and was already prepared to honor the man as the greatest officer he had ever served with. Major Crittendon's calm, easygoing manner masked a military genius, who knew the army and understood the finely honed weapon it could become.

The men had responded as well, and without even being coaxed, had sharpened their dress, their manner, and their diligence to duty. Already there had been skirmishes with two groups of brigands, hidden in caverns over by the foothills. The Union troops had been deployed expertly, taking no chances, while still managing to bring the full weight and power of their assault to bear with speed and cunning.

Remarkably, with all of their success, not one soldier had yet to get so much as a scratch as a result of the attacks. The Lieutenant could sense an impatient eagerness cloistered beneath the Major's immaculate uniform. This had become more of a crusade than an operation. There was an unseen force driving this man, driving him to the greatness with which he conducted himself, and at the same time charging wildly toward the hidden flame of an adversary greater than his passion could hide.

Tresser knew the ways of warriors. This man, Major Crittendon was a warrior, and would have been a great leader at anytime, anywhere. Command came as easily to him as breathing, with an amazing economy of words being used to describe the most complicated of maneuvers. The Lieutenant wondered where this man had served during these last many years, and how an officer of such ability could have gone unnoticed, and unheard of during the recent conflict. His thoughts were still festering as he approached the command tent, ready to report the readiness of the men who stood patiently beside their mounts eager for the next operation. Their air of anticipation electrified the air. Even the horses seemed to have caught the wave of excitement which drove their masters to heightened awareness.

"Troop ready, sir." Tresser need say nothing more. Crittendon had brought with him a new level for readiness, and the men had come around quickly to meet that new standard. Crittendon simply nodded, and returned the salute. The splendid uniform once again took its place at the head of the column, and with no more discussion the unit went off at a quick trot. The Major rode upright and proper, like a gentleman, like a leader, like a conqueror.

The previous days' exploits had been little more than a dress rehearsal. On this day the true purpose for the precision and valor of the never-before-known Major Crittendon would come to its fruition.

On this day John Cummins, disguised as Crittendon, would lead the U.S. Cavalry against the mountain stronghold of Jacques Benine, the last remaining vestige of the evil hand of Jacob McPhearson. This would be his last chance to set right the terrible wrong that had been done to the lovely young Ginny Stronton, and to so many others like her. Cummins carried that guilt, even if only for his lack of caring for the damage his lust for revenge had unleashed.

Cummins held his hand to his heart, and whispered Ginny's name, like an ancient Grecian warrior pledging himself to his goddess before battle. He had made no plans for his life following this day, this task, this cleansing. They rode out by twos, united in their cause. Well, almost.

Seems there's always some fool who thinks he knows more than the others, and that his purpose in life is to hear himself talk, letting all those around him to be educated as to how things ought to be. It doesn't take long for the rotten egg to start to stink. Having been on his best behavior for the better part of three days now, Private Lester Coombs just couldn't keep his mouth shut any longer. And he didn't.

"I don't see how a fella could wear a uniform that nice and be worth his muster. Real men don't make themselves up all pretty like that. Why even his horse is all prettied up. He may be a thinker, I'll give him that, but it seems to me that he probably spends way too much time looking at himself in mirrors, and not much time being a man." Riding toward the back as he was, Coombs figured that only the two or three men riding near him could hear what he was saying. Talking other men down, and pointing out their weaknesses, made Coombs the bigger man in his own mind.

And he was a big man. He stood better than six feet in his stocking feet, which he had never been known to wash, and was heavily muscled and thick boned, more a gift of heredity than the result of a lifetime of hard work, which he avoided any chance he could.

He was mean and dirty, and bullied anyone he pleased. He'd been married once, but that didn't go so well. She got tired of him hitting her whenever he pleased and she up and shot him. But her aim was bad and he survived, and then he got drafted into the army at the start of the war. He'd been in ever since.

But this new spit and polish Major looked too much the dandy for Coombs to ignore, and he figured that poking fun, along with a good dose of insolence was just the ticket. That ticket was about to get punched.

Major Critendon, aka John Cummins hadn't lived this long in his line of work by not knowing what was going on around him, with the possible exception of the matter with Bo Findley in the train car. But then, that young woman had been quite lovely.

Putting that lapse behind him, Critendon knew that the sort of foolishness that a man like Coombs would dish out could prove to be contagious, causing the other men to not pay attention to instruction, or even worse, to be slow or even hesitant to follow orders. Truth was, Cummins thought the uniform was a bit overdone himself, but Coombs' insubordination could not be tolerated. He ordered the column to halt.

"Lieutenant Tresser! There is a man in the ranks who has taken exception to my uniform, my horse, and my worthiness to my rank. While I might allow his comments on the uniform, his questioning of my manhood is a matter of honor, which cannot go overlooked."

"And above all, I will not allow any disparaging comments about my horse, which serves our nation with pride, and looks far better in its uniform than that man ever will in his." Crittendon had made sure to speak loudly enough for the entire column to hear what he had to say. The men turned to Coombs as one, waiting for the reply that they figured was coming, and it did.

"With all due respect Major, I'll not sit here and be compared to a horse. And furthermore, sir, if you weren't wearing that fancy pants uniform of yours, I'd be happy to come up there and shove those words right back down your throat." The column became dead silent then, even the horses seemed aware of the friction in the air. Crittendon was equal to the moment. He dismounted, handing the reins to a nearby soldier, and removing his hat and shirt, passed them over to the amazed Lieutenant Tresser.

"Alright Coombs, the uniform is gone --- no rank to hold you back. Come on up here and show me that you're more of a man than my horse." The cackles were up on Coombs' neck now. The men around him were anxious to see what all was about to happen. This was going to be the stuff of fireside talk for years to come.

Truth was, having seen Coombs in action a time or two, most of the men figured the Major was in big trouble here, and were wondering how many years Coombs would be spending in the brig after all this was said and done. Still, if you're going to lead men, you'd better be able to back up your talk. The Major had invited it, and now he was about to get it.

Coombs removed his hat, and his side arm, but left his filthy uniform shirt on. He didn't figured he'd even work up a sweat with this fancy pants Major, and was more than willing to take any punishment the army might decide to hand down afterwards. He was sure that with what he was about to do to Crittendon, he'd be a legend for years to come. In Coombs' way of thinking, it would be worth it.

There was a clearing nearby, and the men dismounted, leading their horses over to form a ring around the would-be pugilists. Tressler started to protest, seeing nothing but trouble coming of all of this.

"Watch and learn, Lieutenant. A leader's greatest enemy is weakness. His greatest friend is strength." The Major then walked out and faced the bulk and power of the blustering Coombs. A few of the men were offering words of encouragement and defiance. The two fighters were of about the same height, Coombs having the heavier body, and with about the same arm length for punching. Coombs just had to open his mouth one more time.

"You ready pretty boy? I'm gonna make you eat every word, Major, sir." The last two words were more of a taunt than a salute. The stage was set.

"I'm ready, Private." With that Coombs lashed out with a giant haymaker, swinging savagely at the Major's head, ready to dismember the man with a single blow. Crittendon brushed the arm aside, standing as he was in the classic European boxing stance. Coombs swung two, three, four more times, nearly falling over in the effort, each time going as before, with the devastating blow being turned into a mere whiff of air. The next punch would end the fight. But Coombs didn't throw it.

Crittendon feinted with his left, and then threw a lightning fast right, striking Coombs square to the top of his nose, and just above the eyes. Coombs stopped moving then. He stood still as a post, confused, with eyes that couldn't focus, and arms that wouldn't move. It was though he had become a statue, a sculpture dedicated to all the fools of the world who think too highly of themselves, and of their ability to overcome with ease all those they wish to belittle.

"You there! Drag this man to that tree over there and set him down against the trunk. Leave his canteen where he can find it, and tie his horse off nearby." The dumbfounded soldiers moved at once to obey the Major's orders, and it became quickly apparent that order had once again been restored in the ranks. The Major retrieved his uniform shirt and hat from the Lieutenant, and ordering the men to mount up, shared some words that would stay with these soldiers long after the memory of this fight had faded away.

"Men, what you just witnessed was a clear example of skill and preparation overcoming brute force and emotion. I was far better prepared for this fight than was Coombs, because I've had training, excellent training in the arts of warfare. I intend to use my training to keep you men safe and alive while we go out and fulfill our duty to our country, and to one another. Always look out for the man beside you."

"Coombs acted the fool, he often does. He has pride, and boldness, but he does not match those qualities up with good judgment. That's why he's lying there under that tree. Truth is, he never stood a chance, and I knew it. But when a man goes to running his mouth about things that don't need to be said, especially on a mission as dangerous as this, he puts the entire company at risk, while they're thinking about his words of cleverness, and not of the task at hand. Petty talk gets men killed, needlessly, while the talker usually lives on without a scratch."

"I will not tolerate any more foolishness in the ranks like I heard from Coombs. The next man who acts the fool as he did, I will consider to be a traitor, determined to undermine this mission, and I will shoot him down on the spot." The Major then pulled his pistol from his holster, and without taking aim, proceeded to blow a hole in the canteen laying beside the still lifeless form of private Coombs, some distance away. That message needed no explanation. It was clear to all the men there --- this man could shoot.

The matter being settled, the Major ordered the Lieutenant to line the men up again, and proceed to their objective. The ranks remained quiet as they headed out, once again by twos. The unmoving form of private Coombs, along with his shattered canteen, was all the legend he would ever get. He was left behind, leaning there against that tree, as a tribute to their Major's cunning, and to a lesson learned which would save more than one man's life before this day was through.

# CHAPTER TWENTY-FIVE

The tavern proved to be a far less menacing place than it had been during their previous visit. Ginny and Francine would once again bunk up in a room together, a familiar yet far more comfortable arrangement for the two former captives. Milo and Xander would be standing guard. But Xander was uneasy, and he took Milo outside to talk. Xander explained his suspicions.

"We've been lied to, Milo. I could see it in their eyes when I talked to folks today. And it wasn't the kind of lie like they were trying to swindle us, it was the kind when they're trying to protect us from something. The General has friends everywhere, we know that, but he has enemies too, and more than before, since those raids on Judge Bennet's hoard. Something's happened to him, I'm sure of it, and it isn't good." Milo was quick to add his two cents.

"You're right, I felt it too. It was like they were all anxious to get us out of town, mostly to get Ginny out of harm's way. Did you notice how the longer we were there, the more folks tried to get us to leave town for one reason or another? What are we gonna do?" Xander was the quiet one, slower to act, but faster to finish. Milo was sure his old friend had an idea, with a lot of thinking behind it. Xander made up his mind.

"I'm going back in to Richmond --- tonight. I'm convinced that the General is nearby somewhere, and that he is in trouble. With Ginny out of the way I might be able to use a little gentle persuasion to loosen up a tongue or two. You stay here tonight and get the girls back to Dellmont in the morning and stay there with them. And keep an eye out. I'm not so sure it's all that safe for them there either. Better post some guards." Milo started to protest but knew the futility of his words before he spoke them. His friend was counting on him to do the work of the two of them in watching over the General's daughter. But there was more, and Xander made it a point to say so.

"We all love Ginny, like the little sister we never had. But I've seen the way you and Francine look at one another. If ever I've seen the Lord's hand at work I saw it this morning when the two of you met for the first time. Milo, never let that girl out of your sight again. You need her like the air you breathe. And she needs you too, to help make her whole again--and you're the only one who can do it."

The matter was settled. Milo would take no chances that night. With the girls' permission, he made himself up a bed just inside their room, sleeping on the floor so that the door could not be opened while he lay there. With all those two girls had been through, having a man they trusted with their lives on guard so close by would only help them to sleep more soundly, being now in the safest of hands.

Xander's horse was wore out, so he borrowed one from the innkeeper. It was a big old draft horse, and none too fast, but wise, and strong enough to carry Xander's massive frame, and the General's, too, if need be.

He left for Richmond within the hour.


The snipers were set. The reinforcements were in place. Two of Jacques' guards had already been silenced. The other had not much longer to live. Major Crittendon had once again proven his skill as a tactician.

The Lieutenant and his men were in position to the west of the cave, where the evening sun would confuse any defenders trying to find a target coming from that direction. If things went as planned, the entire affair would be over in seconds.

Crittendon's left hand gave the countdown, one finger at a time. Five, four, three, two, one....

Twelve rifles fired as one, three with visible targets, the rest toward the back of the cave's entrance. Immediately the Lieutenant's squad came running into the cavern, mowing down anyone there, with orders only to spare any woman they saw, unless she threatened them with a gun. There were none present.

Ten men in all had fallen, none of them Army. Jacques' men had not gotten off a shot. The surprise had been complete, the victory without question. Once the all clear was given, Crittendon and his men made their way to the cave's entrance, bringing along a captive, one of the two guards subdued at the beginning of the operation. Crittendon was all business now,

"I don't see Jacques among the dead. Where has he gone? Speak up!" The terrified guard looked down the barrel of the Major's gun and knew at once that this was a question that required an answer---now. Cummins had only the thinnest description of the man called Jacques, and saw that any one of several bodies laying there could be his. It was important that he know the man was dead. So he used an old trick, a very old trick, figuring that the panicked guard would point out Jacques' body straight off if threatened, trying to save his own skin. If not, well, he'd see. As figured, the man spoke right up.

"He's not here. Him and Layland and the girl and some of the others headed back to Richmond three days ago---somethin' about meeting up with some man name French. Layland saw that man back at some farm and came to warn Jacques that he was nearby. I only know that 'cause I heard them talkin'. I don't know nothin' else." He was sweating, and looking at that gun barrel like it was a snake. Seeing what he saw, and hearing what he heard, Cummins knew the man was telling the truth. He quickly regained his identity as Major Crittendon, and started giving orders again. The game had changed.

"Lieutenant, arrange a burial detail for the dead. See if this man can give any names to go with the bodies, and make note of it. Have your men search the place for contraband, and for any livestock left behind. I am going ahead back to camp to write my reports on today's action. If the prisoner gives you any trouble, shoot him. Return when you are certain everything is in order. Good work, Lieutenant." Salutes were exchanged, and Crittendon mounted up and then turned to speak to the Lieutenant once again, this time with a bit of a smile on his face.

"Oh, yes, and Lieutenant, have a couple of men stop by and pick up Coombs on the way back. I'd hate for him to miss roll call in the morning." Crittendon again saluted and then rode off at a good clip. The Lieutenant was pleased that the Major had such confidence in him to leave the important task of securing the site to him. It was something that the Major had done himself in the two previous actions.

It was approaching evening by the time the troop had made its way back to the camp site, hungry and tired, but full of confidence as once again the Major had led them into battle without even one man wounded. It was unheard of. The only apparent casualty was Private Coombs' pride.

The Lieutenant had just dismounted and was barking out orders for the handling of the prisoner when an army courier rode in, presumably with dispatches and such. It was too early in the month for payroll. The rider slowed down and stopped next to the Major's horse which was tied off in the shade of an oak tree not far from the command tent. He seemed confused, and saluted as the Lieutenant approached.

"Good evening, Lieutenant, sir. How is it that the Major's horse is all the way out here? I thought the Major was still in Richmond." The puzzled look on the man's face caught the Lieutenant's eye. This was very curious.

"Do you know this horse, Private?" The Lieutenant was not one to let details go unnoticed. He was suspicious of the Private and his words.

"Every soldier in Richmond knows that horse sir. The Major parades himself around town in that fine uniform of his on top of that horse all day long, just to catch the eye of the ladies. Why I've groomed it a time or two myself. It's a sweet tempered little gelding. I'd love to be able to afford a horse like that. No offense intended, sir. Is the Major around? I have dispatches for the commanding officer in charge."

"Major Crittendon is in the command tent over there. Remember to wait for permission to enter."

"Crittendon? Begging the Lieutenant's pardon, sir, but that horse belongs to Major Winston Benedict, you know, the fellow who got drunk and someone stole his horse and uniform and left him at the back of a stable at a town miles away. It happened the better part of two weeks' ago. I thought just about everyone knew about that. They're planning an inquest and everything over it." Red flags flew up in the Lieutenant's mind. Crittendon's sudden appearance, the stylish uniform, and the magnificent horse. What could have. . .

The Lieutenant quickly made his way over to the command tent, and without hesitation, walked straight in to demand an explanation. And he got it. It was just not the one he was looking for.

Sitting on the Major's cot was the splendid uniform, neatly folded, with his hat and gloves laying nearby. Major Crittendon was nowhere to be found.

# CHAPTER TWENTY-SIX

J acques Benine was a man of great cunning, always a step ahead of those around him. But then such things can be an illusion, especially if those you keep around you prove to be a step slow in life in the first place.

His capturing of the General looked be a stroke of genius. Jacques now knew that it was Stronton who had led the attacks on Judge Bennet's home and office. He did not yet understand the presence of the General on the farm which McPhearson had managed to steal from the O'Dell family, but as he had no interest in farms, and less use for McPhearson, he really didn't care.

So far Stronton had been treated well, bound, and locked away, yes, but no harm had come to him. Jacques was saving that privilege for the real Rue French, whom his informants had seen approaching Richmond earlier that day.

Jacques had no idea that French, disguised as Major Crittendon, had recently wiped out his stronghold back at the cave. Had he been aware, the events of this day might well have turned out very differently than planned.

Already an offer for parlay was being prepared, awaiting French's arrival. One of Jacques' thugs would deliver the note suggesting a chance to settle accounts with the man who had dared to impersonate the notorious Rue French.

The letter of invitation included a sincere apology for any misunderstanding, and the immediate withdrawal of the mistaken death mark and bounty which had been placed upon the life of the man known as Rue French, in response to the actions of the General and his accomplices. With McPhearson nowhere to be found, Jacques saw the opportunity to rebuild his organization with the help of French, and his connections in the North. He rightly assumed that the man controlled large sums of cash which could be used to renew their most profitable mainstays, opium and gambling.

Jacques had no illusions. Rue French was a very dangerous and unpredictable man. This peace offering, using the General as a good faith gesture, would not solidify anything, but might be enough to restore the trust which Stronton's vigilante actions had shattered. Even the honor held among thieves could make a man money.

Jacques looked across the room at his captive, the great Brigadier mounted so majestically on a chair instead of a horse. He imagined the kind of tortures and agonies a man with the reputation of Rue French would unleash upon this upright citizen and pillar of the community.

But in the meanwhile, even captives needed to be fed. Jacques passed the word for Cinnamon, the young woman that he kept around for odd jobs and entertainment as the need arose. Today she would be spoon feeding the great General, treating him to a delicious broth of beef with noodles, his hands being tied behind him, thereby unable to do it himself. Jacques relished the humiliation of it all.


John Cummins was far away from the army encampment by the time Lieutenant Tresser discovered Major Benedict's uniform sitting neatly folded on the cot in the command tent. A quickly-assembled search of the surrounding area found nothing, not even a usable set of horse prints to work by. It was as though Major Crittendon had simply disappeared from the face of the earth.

In many ways he had done just that, especially since Crittendon had never really existed in the first place. It was a credit to the skill of John Cummins, alias Rue French, alias, Major Crittendon, alias again and again and again, that he had once more pulled off the greatest of swindles --- that of being someone else, and getting by with it.

He was riding now for Richmond. If Jacques was still alive, he was as dangerous as ever. There was still a bounty on his head for whoever could find him, and dealing with Jacques meant walking into very unfamiliar territory --- almost.

As Rue French, Cummins had walked the back alleys and the dark corridors of the east coast of America, and in many ways those places were very much like similar haunts known to others hundreds if not thousands of years before. The clothing had changed, as well as the weaponry, but people still had the same desires and weaknesses, and for the most part, the devil's work had remained unchanged.

Jacques would be easy to find, but hard to locate. A word spoken to the right fellow, accompanied by a coin would get a message to just about anyone, just about anywhere. But he who asks is not he who tells, and arranging an ambush for an unknown target, and in his own town to boot, would be difficult at best.

Cummins would be at the disadvantage here. The people who worked for Jacques would be more aware of the bounty than any others, and might be willing to make an attempt for such a handsome sum. Of course, Cummins knew full well that Jacques had no intention of paying even a dime of that reward money to anyone. It was just an easy way to get someone else to do his dirty laundry. When thugs become bosses, they remain thugs just the same. It was one thing when Cummins had come to Richmond two weeks or so before to obtain the information he needed to locate Jacques' hideout. He knew several ways of finding such things out. All it took was a coin or two and some very familiar strong armed tactics. He had always been a very persuasive fellow when the need arose. But actually finding and getting close enough to kill this Jacques fellow, a man he would not recognize if he saw him on the street, was going to be another thing altogether. He needed a go between of some sort, someone who he could trust, who knew Jacques well enough to lead him into a trap. Right now his options were zero.If only Jacques had been at the cave with the rest of his group of thugs! The plan had gone so well, getting the uniform and horse from Major Benedict, buying the written orders under the table from the General's own secretary, convincing Tresser and his men of his identity, and leading three successful raids in four days --- it couldn't have gone any better. Excepting of course that Jacques wasn't where he was supposed to be. And now the army wasn't nearby to add its firepower to the effort. Cummins smiled to himself as he enjoyed the memory of successfully impersonating a high-ranking Union Cavalry officer. He had never been in the army, any army, and had nothing but disdain for the type of nonsense that often goes with it all. He had meant what he said to Stronton --- a butcher's waste of men and money. But he did have to admit how much he had enjoyed and even relished in the role of command during those few days. Leadership had always fallen easy upon his shoulders. He then remembered Priscilla, and who he had been, and what he could have become if only... Maybe someday he'd have another shot at life. Just maybe there was a place for him out there in the real world where he could use his skills in a legal and positive way. Maybe he could still become the man he was always supposed to be. Ginny Stronton had already made a difference in him. Maybe that was the difference he needed.

Thinking of his impersonation of Crittendon made him think of the acting job that General Stronton must have done to pull the wool over the Judge's eyes, and Jacques' as well it seemed. Stronton had actually impersonated him in order to pull off the effort. Saving a young girl from her imprisonment was a noble thing for any man to do --- ballads and poems had been written of such things. He regretted now that he had never done any such noble thing while he was pretending to be Rue French.

And so there it was. On this ride back to Richmond, John Cummins finally had allowed himself to understand the irony of it all, how Stronton's pretending to be Rue French was really no different than his pretending to be Rue French, excepting for all the good done by one man, and all the bad done by the other. If John Cummins was to go on in life, Rue French would have to die, once and for all. It had to be.

He found a farm house as night fell, and paid to stay the night in the barn, making no effort this time for a swindle or a con. Those days were over now, and they needed to stay over. Somehow a straw bed and a coarse blanket felt like the bedroll of a king that night. A man with a clear conscience can feel that way from time to time.

It took the better part of two days to ride back to Richmond, and it gave John Cummins plenty of time to do some high-quality thinking. This would be his last effort --- the elimination of Jacques and the remainder of his outfit. It needed to be done, and he knew that he was just the man to do it. And while he had begun this trek with no thoughts beyond the task at hand, his constant dwelling on the lovely face of Ginny Stronton had caused him to rethink his self-worth, and to consider the truth as it lay --- he needed that girl in his life.

He'd been a fool to leave her like that. He had been such a coward, sneaking off before dawn, showing no respect whatsoever for her feelings in the matter, while trying to show her how much he loved her by playing the noble knight in shining armor. He was a fool.

It was late afternoon when he arrived at a makeshift hotel that had recently been renovated from its earlier calling as a stables. The builders had actually done a pretty good job of it all, and the place seemed solid enough, if peculiarly laid out.

The rooms had been made up right where the horse stalls had stood, long and narrow, with a wide swinging window without glass at the end of each room. The floors were of hard-packed earth, cleaned, leveled, and swept, and all in all as serviceable as most any floor he'd ever stood upon. At least these floors didn't squeak. Cummins had just finished washing up in the basin provided, when a knock came to his newly hung door. Not expecting company, and having not ordered any room service, not that there would be any in a place like this, Cummins unholstered his pistol and quickly threw the door open, expecting nothing but trouble on the other side. Instead, he found a humble looking Black man standing there with a note in one hand and a package in the other. The note was addressed to "Mr. Rue French," as was the package. The man invited Cummins to read the note, and mentioned that he had been asked to wait for a reply. Such things were customary, and Cummins invited the man in and closed the door behind him. Cummins was armed, and the messenger was not. He read the note through three times, making sure he had understood every word as it was written. Rue French was apparently a known commodity in Richmond, Virginia. And now he knew why. Cummins knew the man who had brought him the note as Layland, having seen him not only recently at the General's farm, but perhaps a year or so before up in Baltimore loading a cargo of contraband onto a ship destined for France. He did not recall seeing one of those notorious caskets that day, which would have spelled doom for another young woman much like Ginny Stronton. His stomach churned realizing how easy it had been for such an exchange to be made. He read the note again, stalling for time, knowing that here was a chance once again to get to the ringleader Jacques Benine, the man whom he, playing the role of Major Crittendon, had so recently failed to kill. His masquerade as Crittendon was over now, along with the uniform and the magnificent mount. There was the question as to whether Jacques had made any connection with him and the raid on the cave.

Cummins considered it unlikely that Jacques knew about the action at the cave at all. It was more just a happy coincidence that they had come looking for him on the very day that he had arrived in town looking for this very Jacques. Things couldn't have worked out better. But in another way they couldn't have been much worse. The General's LeMat pistol had accompanied the note, wrapped in the package the messenger held in his hand. This was more than enough proof to persuade him of the truth of the communication --- that Stronton was indeed Jacques' prisoner. Despite assurances given by this man Layland when questioned, Stronton's condition was a matter of great concern. The possibility that this whole thing could be nothing more than an elaborate trap was not lost on a man who himself was so capable of leading others into elaborate traps. But there was more here than met the eye, and sometimes even seeing is not believing.

Cummins decided then and there that loaded guns and open eyes would be a far better tactic in this matter than hemming and hawing around, looking for an advantage. Time was not on his side. At this point he wasn't sure just what game was being played here, let alone the strength of the hand his opponent held. But it seemed that the ante was up, and the cards were already dealt. The bold move would be the best move here.

"Take me to Jacques---now." He could see the hesitancy in Layland's manner, and knew at once that such a move would catch Jacques off guard, expecting some sort of response to his invitation first, with a meeting to be set up for later. Cummins' revolver helped inspire Layland's response.

"Yes, sir, we'll go right now, just as you ask. I'm sure Mr. Jacques will be surprised to see you come to see him so soon in the day." Layland nervously led the way.

"That's right, he'll be surprised. But then, I'd hate to keep a good man waiting."

# CHAPTER TWENTY-SEVEN

X ander rode on through the night and was at the outskirts of Richmond before dawn. His plan was simple---find the General. After that he'd just have to play it by ear. The war had been a lot like that, and Xander was a seasoned veteran at forging victory away from the iron will of the unknown.

The key to finding the General was his horse. This was a large mount, with an appetite to go with it. Men who worked with horses saw horses, even when they weren't really looking at them. For a seasoned hostler, no two horses looked alike, and a horse like the General's could not walk by unnoticed.

The fellow at the second stable he had visited the day before had seemed the most discomforted by his questions. Asking a stable hand about horses, of all things, should not be a cause for discomfort. He went there first.

The man's name was Dorn, and he was older than most stable hands and stronger too from the looks of him. But such things were not a concern for the massive Xander, who had no fear of any man's strength. He walked quickly up to Dorn and slammed him unceremoniously against a nearby stable wall, holding him in place with one arm while pointing a finger at the man's nose with the other.

"Here is your chance to make me happy. Tell me where they have taken General Stronton. We met yesterday and you did not help me. That makes me very unhappy. You need to make me happy---right now." The hostler tried in vain to push away, to move out from under the crushing weight of Xander's massive strength, but it was to no avail.

"If I tell you, I'll have to leave. I won't be able to stay here any more. It won't be safe for me here. They'll kill me." The man was shaking. He meant what he said, he knew his fate if he talked.

"Lead me to Stronton, and I'll guarantee you a home far from here, on the prettiest little farm you've ever seen. We could use a man with your skills, but right now I'm going to find out if we can use a man with your integrity." Dorn understood Xander's words as they were spoken. He had survived the war, and the destruction of the city. But he could not survive the scum which ran with the likes of a man such as Jacques. He knew the path he must choose.

"I'll take you there, but I'm going with you. I'll not be a part of letting a good man die. And I'm holding you to your promise. If I do this thing, I'm leaving with you today, there can be no tomorrow for me here." Dorn had stopped struggling under Xander's massive arm, an unwinable battle at best. Besides, having a big man like that on your side can cause a fellow to a gain a great deal of confidence.

Xander released the man and held out his hand in peace. Dorn took it, and then walked over to a tool box and pulled out a ten pound sledge with a shortened handle. It would be a weapon of great consequence when held in a powerful hand.

They arrived at their destination only a few minutes later.

Cummins followed Layland for the better part of four city blocks, noticing the two other men shadowing them along the way. As operatives they weren't very good, but then if there was a good one, he didn't see him. Something to keep in mind.

The destination was a likely looking brick storage building which seemed to have somehow escaped the destruction which had plagued so much of Richmond at the end of the war. There were masons nearby working on a new structure, but otherwise this end of town seemed pretty much deserted. As they approached the door, French stopped, and ordered Layland to call his two associates to come out of hiding and walk in front of them. Out in the open the two shadowers seemed humbled, and unless a third man could disguise himself as a brick, two was all there were.

French drew his gun as they walked through the door. He found the General sitting in a chair at the far end of the room, obviously bound, but a glance showed him to be none the worse for wear. A man in fancy clothes stood beside him with empty hands, but a gun ready at his belt. Adding the three men who had come in with French, there were now six of Jacques' men there in all, leaving French a bullet short if it came to that. But then he remembered the General's LeMat that he had tucked into his belt as they had left his room. He hadn't checked the loads. The man wearing the fancy clothes then spoke.

"Rue French, I am Jacques Benine, and I am honored by your presence. I apologize for my clumsiness when I allowed this man Stronton to impersonate you at the Judge's office that day. Jacob had given us only the briefest of descriptions, and this man, dressed as he was, along with very convincing documents, convinced us that he indeed was the true Rue French. Once again, sir, I apologize. We should have been far more diligent."

"But as you can see, the gods have been generous, and this man's carelessness gives us an opportunity to make amends for any misunderstandings that we may have between us. I present him to you as a goodwill gift. You may do with him as you wish. And perhaps, later on this evening, we can sit down together at dinner and discuss how we can enlarge our operations in a manner equally advantageous for the both of us." Cummins wasn't paying all that much attention to what Jacques was saying. Whatever he intended by these theatrics, it was imperative that he get the General out of here, and fast. He couldn't imagine why Stronton was there in Richmond in the first place, having no knowledge of the General's plan to kill him to protect his daughter, Ginny. As far as he knew, he and Stronton were on good terms.

Jacques was the man Cummins had come for. He had been the power behind the phony Judge Bennet. It was Jacques, and not Jacob McPhearson that had put that price on his head. This was the man he had missed at the cave, after going to all the trouble to impersonate a major and enlisted the U.S. Cavalry to help with the raid. A bullet or two could fix the problem of Jacques, but the General's fate as well as his own would soon come into question. Stronton was tied up, and would be no help in a fight. French knew he might be able to hold the lot at gunpoint, but then what? He and the General wouldn't make it a hundred yards before Jacques' men would mow them down.

The General's eyes were busy. Cummins couldn't tell just what it was that he was trying to communicate, but the need for speed seemed apparent.

Right now, his best move was to just play along. He had to keep Jacques' attention, and build his trust. He now found himself in exactly the kind of predicament he had so often put others. Jacques had the cards stacked his way here.

"Jacques, I look forward to dealing with this impostor, and I thank you for your foresight in allowing me to take my revenge on him. It will surely go a long way toward healing our relationship. I can see that you are a man of great skill in dealing with matters of importance, and I am certain that we can work out an arrangement that will profit both of us in the future." French needed to get the General untied and out of there---somehow. He decided to try an old theater trick.

"If you would then please assist me, I need this man's face covered with a sack of some sort, and then to have him untied from that chair, but keeping his hands bound behind him. There is a place not far from here with a pond. I'll take him..."

Cummins didn't get a chance to finish his sentence. At that moment the door blew inward in a deafening crash of splintered wood. With a mighty rebel yell, in charged two unstoppable men armed with time honored weapons, Dorn with his hammer, and Xander with a sturdy oaken club he had found on the way---like powerful warriors from an ancient past.

Jacques drew to fire, but Cummins' pistol was already out and spewed two quick shots, one missing, and the other striking Jacques' gun arm just above the wrist. Cummins had been too careful with his aim, trying hard not to hit the General who was sitting not far from where Jacques had been standing.

Jacques squealed in pain, and grabbing his arm, ran quickly through the door behind him and up a flight of stairs and beyond. Cummins turned and recognized Xander, having seen him working in the stables back at the farm. He ducked the blow of one of Jacques' men and delivered a heavy chop of his pistol against the man's face. He then fired two shots, dropping two more, helping to even the odds.

"Get the General out of here!" Cummins' shout was as much a command as it was a real good idea. He tossed the General's LeMat to Xander, and then turned to follow after Jacques, with only one round left in his five shot pistol. Jacques was leaving a trail of blood, aiding Cummins in his pursuit. But the maze of rooms and hallways John was having to wind through made for slow going. Soon enough, the trail, and Jacques, had disappeared.

Xander heard the words Cummins had shouted over the maelstrom, and catching the General's pistol, understood the situation for what it was. If Jacques came back with more men, the matter would be decided quickly. They were fighting on Jacques' home turf now. A strategic retreat was called for.

Xander effortlessly picked up the General, chair and all, and hurried him out of that room of death and on to safety. Dorn guarded the retreat, but no adversaries were left standing against them. Those two powerful men had made a mastery of breaking heads and smashing bodies. Unknown to them, Jacques had now lost his last six retainers, and there would be none left to pursue them. All the king's men had fallen.

Only Jacques himself remained, wounded, dangerous, desperate.

# CHAPTER TWENTY-EIGHT

The pursuit of Jacques was as heroic as it was useless. The man was in his own element, and only once did he appear again as he dove comfortably between buildings and down alleyways. John Cummins had lost the trail.

But Cummins had not gone unnoticed. Stronton, now untied and fighting mad, was just coming out onto the main street when he glimpsed the running form of Cummins as he pursued someone or something more than a block away from where Xander and the General stood. After the briefest of introductions, and with Stronton's blessing, Dorn had already gone back to pack his things and load his wagon. He had more than earned his welcome at Dellmont for his work this day. Xander was a good judge of men.

Cummins had been heading towards the east side of town, and Stronton and Xander followed after him on foot, Xander's horse being too far away to fetch in time. The General was determined to catch up with Cummins, and settle the matter between them once and for all.  It needed to be done.

Jacques' trail had ended somewhere near a park, a pretty little place with a gazebo and a few benches scattered among the trees.  The park was surprisingly intact for having so recently been through a war, and the wearied Cummins ended his pursuit there, gratefully sitting down on a bench to catch his breath.

He might just as well, for Jacques was nowhere to be found.  He could be just about anywhere.  But he certainly was not there.

Cummins relaxed, and taking a deep breath, looked around at the trees and plants surrounding him, their leaves rustling in the gentle breeze.  He thought again about Ginny, and the beauty of Dellmont, and his purpose for being there in the first place---to kill Jacques Benine.  It would be autumn soon, and those same trees would be changing colors.  This was a pretty little place, and he chided himself for not stopping more often at all the other pretty places he had seen in his years of travels, and for not taking the time to enjoy the simple gifts of nature.  He was tired of running, by foot, by horse, by carriage, by train...

He let himself get a little more comfortable and decided he'd just set a spell.  A man like Jacques would surface again some where, some time.  He had no need to be looking under rocks.  It could be done another day.

He noticed three other people in the park, strolling comfortably among the plantings without a hurry in their life.  John Cummins enjoyed the peace and quiet.  Perhaps he should go on back to Dellmont and visit with Ginny for a time.  He regretted now leaving the way he had, without a goodbye, or even a "by your leave." He let his mind drift back to her now --- her smile, her laugh, her kiss.

He wasn't paying attention. He was being watched. This park had somehow become a magnet for all those who knew Rue French, and wanted him dead. And he had been found.

Stronton and Xander were at the edge of the park now, and could clearly see John Cummins sitting on a park bench, seemingly without a care in the world. The General stopped and surveyed the scene. Something wasn't right here.

Xander agreed. There was no way that Cummins would leave himself out in the open like that. It wasn't his way. Maybe he was setting a trap, with himself as bait. There were three other people in the park, but none of the three seemed to offer any sort of a threat. Two walked together, enjoying the afternoon air, and the third, a man in brown clothing seemed to be busy looking for nuts or some such on the ground below him. Jacques was nowhere to be seen.

Still, Stronton wasn't convinced. He and Xander would come up quietly, and see if they could get Cummins' attention. What he had to say to this man needed to be said face to face. The General checked the loads in his LeMat pistol, Xander having explained how it came into his possession during the fight.

They moved in closer.

"There is no fool like your own fool."

John Cummins could remember hearing his Granddaddy's voice saying those words just as sure as if he'd been standing next to him right then and there. And he would be right, Grand-dad was most always right, having lived long enough to know right from wrong and everything in between.

Of course, Grand-dad was dead and gone now, years ago, but his wisdom lingered. And Cummins could only shudder to think what the old fellow would make of the way little Johnny had managed to ruin his life over a girl. It seemed that John Cummins was immune to just about everything this world could throw at him---except for women. There, in one word, was the sum total of ruin in his life---his inability to deal with women. And it was all his own doing.

He had already built a shrine for Priscilla long before she had left him. She was so very beautiful, so amazing to behold, with lips that told lies, and eyes that hypnotized. What a fool he was to think that he could keep such a vision all to himself, a woman accustomed to having so many suitors worshiping her.

He had spent time with other women since then, women whose company was bought and sold in any of a dozen forms of exchange. They used him up until only the shell of John Cummins had remained, a shell which had been filled by another highly successful fool--Rue French --- a legend whose notorious partnership had brought Cummins great wealth, and greater misery.

Would he trade it all for a steady wife, a couple of kids, and forty acres to plow? Not a chance. Sooner or later he'd leave her, in mind if not in body. He could not remain faithful to a bargain he had no desire to make.

Helen Williams was pretty, and fair, and a dead shot with a rifle---which she would probably end up using on him in time. She had a lovely face and a lovely form, and the intimacy required in keeping her alive had nearly caused him to lose his senses and stay under her spell. But it was no accident that he had left her side. Was his rendezvous with Jacob McPhearson so important that he would rather be with him than with her? He knew better. He left because he wanted out. She was love-ly---but after knowing a woman like Priscilla, lovely just wasn't enough. There were pretty girls everywhere.

He should have never left Ginny. With her it was differ-ent. He loved her. She understood him, and wanted him there with her, not running out on this fool errand. That's why he had left so early in the morning---she would have never allowed it. And why was the General here in Richmond, and how did a man like Jacques capture him? Had Ginny sent her father after him to bring him back? It was something to think about. He needed to find the General and talk with him.

He'd been sitting there on that park bench for quite a while now, not common for a man such as himself. For him it was never a good idea to stay too long in any one place, at any time. It made him too easy a target. He needed to get moving.

And so John stood up and straightened out his coat. It was time to go home, home to Ginny. Let Jacques stew in his own juices for a time. He would deal with him later.

Cummins felt the sharp punch of the bullet long before he heard the report of the gun. He'd been a fool. Staying too long in one place, thinking about the woman he loved, instead of staying home with her, home. . .

The next slug caught the back of his head just as he reached to pull his pistol. He would make no defense this day, his luck pouring out of him along with his blood, as his lifeless body hit the ground hard and did not move again. He had not heard the report of the gun that time, or of the voice of the man who now stood over him, the triumph of his words speaking louder than the words themselves.

"Thanks to you, Rue French, I am now a very wealthy man---a very wealthy man indeed." The fox had been run to ground.

Sheriff Samuel Hoskins stood there over the lifeless body of his victim, gun still drawn, dollar signs in his eyes. Ever since that day at Zachariah Shartle's farm, that day that found him bleeding with a wound to his leg after bullets had rained into that unsuspecting household, he'd held a grudge for the man the ambushers had called 'Rue French.' It was later that week, when visiting with the railroad detective who had fought off the attackers there with him, that he learned that the man known as Rue French had a bounty of $10,000, a life's fortune for a man making small town Sheriff's wages.

And French was a known killer, wanted for robbery and thievery in several states. The only problem---no one had been able to give the name a face. Until now. And so Hoskins carefully formed his plan as he waited for his leg to heal sufficiently to ride again.

It wasn't difficult to stalk this man French, not with the trail of bodies the fellow left in his wake wherever he went. Of course, the badge helped. Folks would open up to a lawman in pursuit of a known killer. Information had been easy to come by. When he got word of a man meeting the description having been in and around Richmond, the rest was simply a matter of watching and waiting. He was good at watching, and the waiting had been worth the prize.

$10,000. He was a wealthy man! All Hoskins needed to do now was to find this Jacques fellow he'd heard so much about and collect his reward. He'd been careful not to tip his hand, and had as of yet made no inquiries concerning Jacques, or his whereabouts, but he was certain that once word of Rue French's death got out, Jacques would beat a path to the his door to see the body, the price for the viewing a mere $10,000. It had been easy money.

"You there!" Hoskins heard the voice behind him. It was a Southern voice, deep and powerful---the voice of a man used to giving commands. He smiled. Whatever the fellow wanted, the gun in his hand and the glimmer of the star on his vest should do more than enough to quiet him down. This was his way, in charge, always in charge.

The Sheriff turned, gun in hand and wearing his most professional face, expecting to overwhelm this sightseer with his importance. It was a mistake he would not live to regret.

Hoskins felt a tug at his coat, like a bee sting, but growing in pain, as blood started to stain his shirt. And then came another---but this was no bee. He looked again, trying to find a target, someone who would have the audacity to fire his weapon on a lawman wearing a badge. There behind him he saw his answer.

The tall man stood there holding his LeMat pistol, assuming the stance of a duelist, with a look of hatred in his eyes. The Sheriff tried to lift his heavy pistol, to reply in kind to this blackguard, but the LeMat blew fire again, and now the Sheriff's arm refused to move. He fell to his knees, weakened and dazed. Numbness took over, and his leg somehow no longer hurt. Hoskins smiled at his folly, and his station in life --- he would die a rich man.

Hoskin's empty eyes stared upward at the Brigadier General with his white coat and broad billed hat. The Sheriff's badge was removed and secreted away. This man had no jurisdiction here in Richmond, neither here, nor in the next destination his soul was undoubtedly destined for.

"Xander! There's a rooming house just down the street. Get Cummins over there and see what you can do to stop the bleeding. I'll see if I can round up a doctor somewhere. We've got to save this man! Hurry!" Xander had no difficulty lifting up the motionless body of John Cummins, and went off at a trot toward the nearby boarding house. There would be no argument tolerated from the proprietor, what with Xander's imposing stature and the General's gold to dissuade any hesitancy to take in the wounded man.

Within the hour the General had returned with the only doctor he could find, a woman of all things, who upon being questioned of her skills and training for such a profession, had pulled a lethal looking pistol from her case and pointed it directly at the General's midsection.

"Say another word like that mister and I'll give you the privilege of finding out just how well I can dig a .44 slug out of your gut. But you'd have to wait while I tended to your friend first." Stronton decided not to challenge a woman with a gun, at least not while it was pointed at him, and not at such close range. He knew full well that women and guns were a dangerous combination---a man never knew when either one might go off, accidentally, or on purpose.

Xander had wisely appropriated a room on the bottom floor of the boarding house, and had managed to quickly silence the landlord's objections using his imposing form, along with a strategically placed coin to the fellow's hand. Xander later apologized for his rudeness, accompanied by a few more coins, more than enough to smooth a few ruffled feathers.

The Doctor set her black leather bag down on the floor near the bed and took a quick look at her patient's face. Her expression changed for a few seconds, but then she went back to work. The scalp wound was serious, but the bullet had somehow glanced off. A very hard head she mused. The wound to the shoulder still held the slug, but seemed to have missed the main artery. She ordered Xander and the General to completely undress the man and lay him face up. The General objected.

"We should at least leave him his underwear---it isn't decent!" The Doctor just smiled and paid no attention to his concerns.

"There's no need for modesty here, gentlemen. I've seen John Cummins this way before. It seems he just can't stay out of trouble." She got busy sanitizing her tools in the boiled water the maid had brought for the purpose, while the astonished men worked quickly to follow the Doctor's wishes.

John Cummins' luck hadn't run out yet.

# CHAPTER TWENTY-NINE

J acques leaned against the alley wall, satisfied that he had out-foxed his pursuers. The only one that he had seen chasing him was Rue French, but he assumed that the other two men, the ones who had burst through the doorway, were after him as well. His arm ached from the bullet wound, but no bones seemed to have been hit, and he was confident, knowing that he had survived knife wounds worse than this in times past.

He dared not go back to the warehouse where he kept a room, figuring that there would be someone there waiting for him---someone waiting to kill him. But there was another place, a secret place nearby, to which there was a back entrance that passed through a bakery---a place known to only a very few.

A minute or two later Jacques could smell the wonderful aroma of fresh baked bread, admittedly one of his weaknesses in life. As he went through the back of the building, he grabbed up a hot loaf and took it with him. It wouldn't be missed.

His destination was a small apartment, hidden from the rest of the building by a skillfully designed passage, which itself lay hidden behind a storeroom wall. The room was sparsely furnished, but filled from floor to ceiling with all manner of masks and bones and items of strange design and questionable origins. This was the home of Sellah, a Priestess of Wonder by her own accounts, but known as a witch to most everyone who knew her at all. She held the secrets of the ages, with potions and serums from the dark corners of the earth. She held power over others. Sellah was a woman of mystery.

Jacques disliked this place of sorcery, but he had come here from time to time to enjoy the pleasures of a drug in-duced sleep, or the amazing shapes and designs the burned incense could create in his mind when combined with forbid-den drink. But this day he had come to Sellah for healing, and to a hiding place where none would find him.

Jacques carefully walked in, and sat down before a pecu-liar altar as was expected of him. This was an altar far more familiar to those who understood the rituals of Egypt, than those of the churches of Europe. Sellah suddenly material-ized before him, a skill she was known for, and in a manner which no one understood.

"Why are you here Jacques? Your wound is not serious, and could be bandaged elsewhere. What is it you wish of Sellah?" Her voice was as thin and wistful as the smoke which rose from the tallow candles. She moved with a catlike grace which defied her age, a woman well into her eighties by all ac-counts, and yet bearing the shape and countenance of a wom-an much younger, her form easily seen through her flimsy loose fitting garments. It was said that she was of Spanish origin. It was said that she could speak to the dead. It was said that she could fly.

"That man Rue French betrayed me and came up shooting. He had brought a gang of at least eight men against us, and we were hopelessly outnumbered. He got off a lucky shot and hit my arm. I've come not only for the wound, but for a place to hide for a few days until I can safely leave town." Jacques tried not to show his fear to her.

She did not move, and the expression on her face did not change. Something was very wrong, and knowing a woman like this, one who knew everything about everything, he feared that she saw through his cowardice, a veil as thin as her clothing.

"First we will bind your wounds. And then I will send you out to choose a fowl to be sacrificed, an offering to Anubus for the safety of your soul, and to gird you for the battle yet before you. But use caution, only one bird is intended for you this day, and only it holds the power required to restore your rightful place in this world. Choose the wrong bird, and the sacrifice will be for naught. It will mean your death."

It took only a few minutes for Sellah to cleanse and bind Jacques' arm, using potions and creams which quickly dulled the pain, and promised a rapid recovery. Then it became his task to go out into the fenced yard and choose from among the many chickens and ducks which she kept there, supporting herself through the sale of eggs and live birds for the many stew pots there in Richmond.

The local folks were used to seeing Sellah, who they all knew as "the Chicken Lady", out in the yard wearing overalls and a straw hat most any time of the day. Only a very select few knew of her closely guarded secrets. These few knew the terrible price that loose tongues would bring down upon them. Her secret was kept.

Jacques was convinced that much of what Sellah said and did was little more than a carnival act, and that her appearance of youth was more than likely a nod to a lie as to how old she really was. A good lie could go a long way. He should know.

Out in the chicken pen, Jacques didn't see the reasoning that one bird was destined just for him. They all looked pretty much alike. He reasoned instead that whichever bird he could catch with his injured arm must certainly be the one for him, and went to work. A few minutes later he returned with his specially chosen chicken.

"Is this indeed the sacrifice meant for you?" Sellah always used that funny far away voice when she was doing things like this. Jacques saw it all as just part of the act. He'd go along as needed.

"Yes, Sellah, I am certain that this is the one." The bird had not yet stopped quivering and flopping its wings. Jacques just wanted to get this over with.

"Very well, Jacques, your fate is now in your hands. Let the sacrifice begin."


The tribute to Anubus, and the ministrations with the chicken took the better part of an hour, during which time Jacques was required to drink all manner a foul-tasting brews, and to wear the chicken's feathers on his scalp. Finally, a drop of his blood was mixed with that of the chicken and burned on the small metal altar.

When all was said and done, the tribute to Anabus complete, they finished plucking the bird and fried it up in a skillet over the fire. Sellah might have been a priestess of the dark arts, but she was unwilling to waste a perfectly good chicken just because it had been offered to Anubus this day. It was delicious.

Jacques would stay sequestered there for several more days, at least until the moon had completed its cycle, and the time would be right for him to exact his revenge upon his betrayer. He must not fail.

# CHAPTER THIRTY

Xander came charging back through the Delmont gate late the next day, the horse lathering, and the rider exhausted. Stronton's instructions had been very clear---bring Ginny back to Richmond---fast!

Ginny waited patiently as Xander finished his report of the events of the last few days, his rescue of the General, and the circumstances surrounding the wounding of John Cummins, and of his desperate battle to stay alive.

Xander had traveled all night, but was still ready to find another horse and return at once. But after taking a look at the big fellow, Milo put his foot down and ordered him to stay put and get some sleep. As far as they knew Jacques was still out there, and a sleepy man would be less protection for the General and his daughter than they might be needing back in Richmond. Xander couldn't argue the point, not with Milo of all people, so he didn't.

Minutes later the hastily prepared carriage left Dellmont once again, just as it had only a few days earlier. But the circumstances were very different now. The General was safe and secure, and out of the hands of the notorious Jacques. John Cummins, however, was in a bad way. For Ginny, the horse couldn't go fast enough.

And it couldn't. Milo was no beginner in these matters, and he knew that Richmond was a long way off. Leaving late in the day as they were, there was no way they would reach Richmond before nightfall. It was one thing for the mighty Xander to travel along the back roads of Virginia through the night in a desperate effort to bring Ginny back to the side of the man they all knew she loved. It was quite another to make the same trip in a carriage, and with a lady along for the ride.

Hours later, Milo and Ginny stopped once again at the tavern they had seen all too often as of late. It was quite late, and the innkeeper was none too anxious to open the door to Milo, but Ginny's insistent voice, and a little persuasion from the innkeeper's wife was all it took to get them in for the night.

There were no rooms available, but the fire was warm and with Milo nearby, Ginny would be in no danger in the main room this night. The other men sleeping there were courteous, and moved away from where the girl would be sleeping.

Ginny had Milo up and going at first light. As always, the horse could not go fast enough.

Helen Williams had spent the night in the room sitting near her patient. The overstuffed chair in the corner had not been nearly as comfortable toward the early morning hours as it had seemed the night before. This was now the morning of the third day of Cummins' recovery, and while the wound to his shoulder was healing nicely, the wound to the back of his scalp was worrisome.

That bullet had struck hard, but had only creased an inch or two along the scalp. But the impact had apparently knocked Cummins out cold, and he had not awakened since. Forcing liquids down his throat was difficult and risky, the chances of him drowning on a well-meant cup of water was not without precedent.

Helen wished then that her father was there to lend advice. But the venerable Doctor was up in Pennsylvania, and even if a message could find him yet today, this patient would most likely be dead before he got there. It would be up to her and her alone. John Cummins had saved her life back at the Shartle farm, and not all that long ago. It had fallen to her now to do the same for him. But how?

She sat back down in that big overstuffed chair to renew her watch. An old dog-eared Bible sat nearby, and she opened it up to pass the time. She had always enjoyed the Psalms, they brought her peace and strength on those days when she needed it the most.

This was one of those days.

Ginny and Milo had renewed their journey shortly after first light, but not without discussion. Ginny wanted to leave sooner, but Milo, always the well of wisdom, would have none of it. He demanded that they eat a good breakfast before they left. After all, the meal was part of the price for the lodging. A little extra was packed away for the road.

But more so, Milo knew full well that John Cummins, the man Ginny loved, might well be dead and gone by the time they got there. Xander had been very detailed about the severity of the wounds Cummins had suffered, and Milo, a veteran of years of war and of its wounded, knew that this sort of thing usually went very badly. The girl would need her strength in either case.

Ginny was a nervous wreck, and after a time asked Milo to join her in the carriage and drive, his horse being tied off to the back. She talked and talked to her friend and protector, explaining her thoughts and working out her emotions.

"Milo, I know it all probably looks wrong, but I can't help it. Maybe it's because of all I've been through, or maybe it's because I don't want to have to pretend anymore. For whatever reason, the whole debutant-courting thing just doesn't appeal to me. It's all so silly, with its rules and etiquette and parties and punch bowls. I never have been one for frilly dresses and such, and I can't imagine that I ever could be." She stopped for a moment, took a breath, and went on.

"I so wish Mama was here. She was so wise, and knew me so well. You knew Mama back when I was a little girl. What do you think she would say about all of this?" She was putting Milo on the spot here, hoping for some answers, hoping for some encouragement. Not knowing who else to turn to. Milo smiled, and just told her.

"I knew your Mama before you were even born young lady, and to tell the truth, if I hadn't watched you growing up all these years, I'd swear here and now that you were her sitting right here beside me. And I'm here to remind you, and your hard head, that if you had accepted the offer that several folks extended to you to take you in after your Mama passed, instead of staying there in that old house by yourself, a lot of the troubles you've suffered in the last year or so would never have happened. I know why you stayed, and how you wanted to keep the place up until your Daddy came back, but other folks saw trouble, and they were right. You need to pay more attention to what other folks know, and learn by it."

Ginny sat silent then, and understood the depth of Milo's words. She was hardheaded, and had always been proud of her independence. McPhearson's men had caught her alone and off guard. She had no real idea what was in store for her as their captive, always figuring that she would have the chance to get free sometime when they weren't looking. But that time never came. She was drugged, she was moved around, and she was used for pleasure. There was no escape.

In the days when she should have been dressing for parties, she was being held captive in a brothel. At a time when young men should have been calling on her, they were dying on the field of battle. The fates had been unkind to her--- some of it her fault, some of it not. But all of it had worked to shape the woman she was this day. She was who she was, and not likely to change much because of someone else's advice. It wasn't enough.

"Milo, you haven't answered my question. What would Mama say?" Milo sat there, holding the reins, trying to figure the right words to say. He really couldn't get his tongue to work in step with his head, so he just blurted it out.

"Alright, Ginny Stronton, here it is. I've already told you just how much you are like your mother, and there's no way you'll ever really know that since you aren't old enough to remember back to when she was you. There were a lot of folks who didn't think your Daddy was good enough for her, and her folks, your Grandparents, even went so far as to forbid the marriage. She ran off and became Mrs. Henry James

Stronton anyway, and figured she was going to let herself be happy whether anyone else wanted her to be happy or not. And she was. And you are the happy, strong, and wonderful result of that decision."

"A weaker woman could have never gone through what all you did, and come out as well as you have. It's gonna take Francine a longer time to get her life back in order again, and I hope I'll still be part of her life when that happens. She's a fine girl, and looks up to you for courage and inspiration." Ginny was amazed by Milo's words, and never knew that her mother had run off with her Daddy. Just thinking of it made her smile.

"You still haven't answered my question. What would my Mama say if I told her I wanted to be married to a man that had been a thief, and a killer, and didn't even use his own name to do his business?" She looked at Milo with those ornery brown eyes of hers, those same eyes that she had employed growing up, when she was finagling a piece of rock candy from a soft hearted friend.

"She would have said, 'Go ask your father'. And since you know that your father was the one who sent Xander back to fetch you as quick as possible so that you could be there by this man's bedside, you already have your answer. What I can't figure out is why you're taking so long to get there."

Ginny grabbed the reins from Milo's hands and stopped the horse at once. There was no mistaking the look on her face, or her determined posture as she moved toward the center of the seat.

"You need to get back on that horse of yours now, sir. This carriage will go much faster without your weight slowing it down. I'll see you in Richmond!" The exchange of glances and smiles told the rest.  Soon enough came the snap of the whip and the carriage was away, heedless of the holes in the road or the punishment the old buggy was forced to endure. Ginny would ride the horse bareback if necessary.  She needed John Cummins in her life.  She needed to be with him, now.

# CHAPTER THIRTY-ONE

Henry Stronton tried to stay busy, fiddling with the horses and generally getting in the way. From time to time he would come into the room, presumably to check on Cummins' progress, but always finding a reason to stay and talk with the attractive young lady Doctor.

He liked Helen. She was very bright, and didn't take any of his nonsense. It was good to have a woman around to talk to again. It just wasn't the same with Ginny, although a woman she had become. This was different, and he somehow felt younger again.

He helped Helen with changing the sheets, Cummins' bulk being difficult to manage for the girl. He even got the Doctor to step out of the house with him for a breath of fresh air from time to time. But she was always uncomfortable, unsettled, happy to be with the General, but always worried about her patient, John Cummins, a man she owed so much to, without his ever knowing it. Her walks with Stronton seldom lasted for much more than an hour.

In truth, Stronton didn't want to be out all that long either. He too had a great concern for Cummins' condition, and the circumstances which had caused his injuries. Originally the General had left Dellmont and come to Richmond to find Cummins, and to kill him. That was his plan. But he had lost some of his resolve before he even left home, listening to Ginny's arguments concerning her feelings for this man formerly known as Rue French.

But he had left for Richmond anyway, bull headed and stubborn, determined as to just how right he was in the matter. Then came that evening at the home of Ben Chalmers, a man that Stronton still called 'lieutenant', where his old friend had put the uncomfortable truth of the matter right before the General's eyes, right where he couldn't help but see it.

By the time Stronton got to Richmond, he knew he had been wrong, trying to force Ginny into being happy by plotting to destroy the very source of her happiness. He'd been wrong, and he was willing to admit it. When he got to town, he had looked for Cummins, hoping to settle matters and bring the man back to his daughter. But it never happened.

It seems that Jacques Benine, the butler who guarded the Judge's office so carefully, was on the look out for the real Rue French, John Cummins himself, when the imitation Rue French, Stronton, appeared on the streets making inquiries. The General was taken at gunpoint, and held hostage, awaiting the opportunity to be dealt with by the real Rue French, and to heal old wounds between French and Jacques.

And now Stronton owed John Cummins his life. He didn't know how Cummins had found him, and only now had found out that Xander's sudden appearance had nothing to do with whatever plan Cummins was hatching during those desperate moments before the door had suddenly come crashing down.

He had almost gotten to the place where Cummins had been sitting on that park bench, when that man wearing the badge pulled his gun and shot John down, making no effort to take him alive. This is what had prompted Stronton's re-action, and caused him to shoot that man in turn, without forethought, or concern for the man's badge. He needed John Cummins to live. He needed for Ginny to hold on to the happiness this man had brought to her life.

And right now he needed Helen Williams to be a great doctor.

And the young woman doctor was doing all she could. Helen had been up and out of her chair every half hour, checking on her patient, and trying unsuccessfully to bring him back to consciousness, somehow to stir him back to this world, and away from wherever it was he had gone to. Nothing seemed to work. It was late in the day, and her frustration was building. She was having trouble maintaining her focus.

She had been reading the Psalms, mostly without notic-ing the words, when the book fell open to a different page. Without caring, she sat back down and continued reading, but not really reading at all. What to do?

Then, as though an angel had come and marked the place, a single passage leaped out of the text to her, giving direction, giving permission. She read the passage again, and then again. Her heart ran faster as she suddenly knew what she must do. It had to be done. She marked the verse, whispered a prayer of thanks, and got busy.

It was insanity, it was not allowed. But lying in his present state, John Cummins would soon waste away to nothing, and, even if he somehow survived, would only be a shell of his former self. Better he were dead than a mere carcass decaying in a bed meant for the living. He deserved better. It was up to her to do what needed to be done.

She stood up, and walked over to where she had left her leather bag, a bag filled with medicines and lotions meant for healing. But instead, Helen pulled out the all too familiar pistol, the same weapon with which she had playfully teased the man they had once called Rue French just weeks before. Her mind was made up. There could be no turning back. This then was her final prescription.

Helen walked over to where John Cummins lay, motionless, unaware of his surroundings, and kissed him gently on the forehead. She checked the load, and brought the pistol's barrel within inches of his head, just to the right of his ear. Helen once again breathed a quick prayer, and carefully pulled back the hammer. She then closed her eyes, and squeezed the trigger.

# CHAPTER THIRTY-TWO

The pace had been blistering, but Ginny and Milo found themselves on the outskirts of Richmond in only a few hours. Xander's directions to the rooming house were excellent, just as Milo expected they would be, and within minutes they were past the park and tying the horses off to the post in front. The steps up to the door were a bit worn, but Ginny scaled the loose bricks like a deer. Just as they were preparing to knock on the weathered oaken door, they were startled by the report of a gun, a pistol of large caliber from the hearing of it, the blast clearly heard through an open window nearby.

The courtesy of a knock was forgotten, as Milo drew his weapon and went barging through the unlocked door, prepared to deal with whatever threat might be hiding behind those walls. In the second downstairs room, he found his answer.

There standing by the bed was a woman with blond hair, holding a pistol down by her side, the smell of gun powder still present in the room despite the open window nearby. She turned her head toward her newly arrived guests and smiled.

"You must be Milo, and you'd be Ginny. Please come in. There's someone here who'll be mighty anxious to see you, young lady." The woman had made no threat with the pistol, but Milo kept his weapon unholstered until he knew what all was going on here. Xander had mentioned a doctor, but didn't say anything about a woman. Ginny walked around Milo's unmoving form, and went quickly to Cummins' side, while Helen slowly turned to put the pistol back into her leather kit bag, her sense of satisfaction clearly seen in her smile.

"Ginny?" That one word, his first word spoken in days, summed up the volumes of words filling his soul, waiting impatiently to be spoken aloud, to be shared and lived at last, chapter and verse. Helen went back over to where the Bible still lay, open to the page and passage which had changed everything. She read the verse out loud to herself, if for no other reason than to acknowledge a power greater than any medicine she would ever use, or cure she would ever find.

"They have ears, but they hear not." Reading it again now she realized that this had nothing to do with healing the sick or brandishing pistols, and she couldn't imagine how she could ever explain how those words had ever encouraged her to do what she did. But she knew now that sometimes suggestions can come from unexpected places to those who are willing to hear. She marked the page with a slip of paper, and slid the book into her case---a new and useful tool to add to the medicines and lotions of her daily work --- right there next to her .44.

She couldn't wait to tell the General all about it when he returned. He had promised to take her to dinner that evening to chat further about her ideas for a clinic. They had become quite close by now, and it seemed that Stronton would very possibly fill a very important role in this young woman's life, and she in his.

Time passed quickly as Cummins, his faculties still not totally working, tried to make some sense of what all had happened to him in these last many days. He remembered pursuing Jacques, he remembered collapsing exhausted on the park bench, he remembered the pain in his shoulder, but nothing after that.

But while he knew Ginny, and the time he had spent with her, he didn't seem to remember Helen, or his time with her at the Shartle farm. It was clear that he was still in a haze, and Helen recommended that they allow him to rest as much as possible. A special meal for the patient had already been ordered up to the land lady. But the young doctor had other, more pressing concerns now --- matters that required immediate attention. Things that could wait no longer.

"Ginny, you and I need to talk. Would you come over to my room for a moment, please?" Ginny didn't much like the idea of leaving John alone like that, but Milo volunteered to sit and watch, and encouraged Ginny to leave the room for a while. Ginny submitted, and went to the room that Helen had arranged for herself just across the hall, a room she had actually spent very little time in.

Helen closed the door behind them, preoccupied with the importance of the things she had to say to this girl that she had never met before today, and yet knew so much about. This was going to be difficult. She poured each of them a glass of cool water, and when they were both seated, Helen started in.

"Ginny, your father has shared a great deal with me about you in the last several days, and I must say that you are certainly a lot prettier than he had led me to know. But that's just an observation on my part. I really brought you here to talk about John Cummins, and our mutual interest in him." Ginny shuddered a bit at that. She had no idea who this woman was, or the role she had played in John's life. She was on the verge of striking out at Helen in anger, but held back to hear what this lovely young blond doctor had to say for her self.

"It was a little more than a month ago that John and I were together at a farm up in Pennsylvania. My father, the Doctor, and I, were there to treat him after he had been injured in an explosion. Amazingly, he was suffering from a head wound then too. He seems to have a head of granite."

"While I was there, some men came and tried to kill him. I was wounded in the fight, and John saved my life. During the process of it all, he got a pretty good look at me while he doctored me up. In my delirium I told my father that I intended to marry John. I'm not sure how much I really meant by that. He's handsome and dashing, and I'd been hurt by a man like that before. I guess I was just trying to deal with the intimacy of it all. But the fact is, nothing really happened between us."

"The thing is, I don't know how much of any of that he remembers. After I shot that pistol next to his ear, and that worked really well by the way, he saw my face, but didn't seem to recognize me. But he knew you as soon as you came in the room. Your father told me that the two of you had spent a great deal of time together there at Dellmont, and he feels that a very special relationship had developed between the two of you. From what I can see, I think it's much more than that. I'll have to admit that when you two were together holding hands a few minutes ago I was a little bit jealous, not wanting any man to prefer another girl over me. You understand, I'm sure. That's just me being me."

"But the fact is, and the real reason why I asked you to come into the room here with me, is that I need your permission for something I want to do."  Ginny looked at this woman, who was really only a few years older than she, and wondered at what all had happened between her and John before he had arrived at her home. She found herself being a bit jealous herself.  But this woman had saved John's life, and brought him back to her again.  She owed Helen that much.

"Helen, I really can't imagine what I could do for you here, you've obviously done so much for John already.  But if you're going to ask me to step aside and let you have free rein with him, I won't go along. I love him, and I intend to keep him in my life for as long as I live."  Ginny's brown eyes were turning green with jealous envy.  She wasn't going down without a fight, with pistols, or spears, or knives as needed.

Helen looked at the intensity of the young woman sitting across from her and smiled from ear to ear. She could see a lot of her father in young Ginny, and she loved it.

"No, you silly girl---John is yours, all yours, and heaven help any woman who would dare try to stand between the two of you.  But you'll have to admit, he is very handsome, and quite a catch. You are a very lucky girl."  Ginny looked at Helen in amazement. This wasn't what she was expecting at all. She let the fighting fur lay down again on the back of her neck, wondering now what it must be that Helen wanted her help with. That answer was coming right then and there.

"I want your permission and blessing to marry your father. I love him so much, he's such a wonderful man, and we've grown very close in these last few days. He's like a gift from heaven, and I feel like he's rescued me from myself. I know this is sudden, but I know it's right."

Ginny could see the tremble in Helen's lip, the difficulty in asking this thing hanging heavy upon her. It seemed like an eternity, but in truth only a few seconds passed by. And then Ginny remembered the audacious words of her lifelong friend Milo, what he had told her on the way there that morning. Ginny smiled.

"You already know the answer Helen, and it's really nothing you need my permission for. Instead, you should ask my father." Ginny giggled then, that wonderful giggle of hers that everyone knew, and went over to give Helen a long loving embrace. Helen was a fine young woman, one to be proud of. Her mother was not coming back, and her Daddy needed someone around, someone to talk to, someone to walk with in the garden. Someone for him to love.

Before it was over they had both been crying happy tears and Helen excused herself to go clean her face before the General showed up. The talk between them never stopped after that, not until Stronton finally arrived with the carriage to take Helen to dinner. His reunion with Ginny was brief, and the only word Helen gave about Cummins was that he was doing much better. Helen took the older man by the arm and whisked him away to the carriage. She was lighthearted and happy, having managed to pass two very important tests that day --- with John, and with Ginny --- and passed them both with flying colors.

Ginny stood by the door and waved as they left. Richmond, once a place of terror and shame for Virginia Stronton, had suddenly become the happiest place on earth.

# CHAPTER THIRTY-THREE

Helen sat close to the General on the way in to town. She had made it past her biggest hurdle---Ginny, and the rest now was up to her.  Suddenly, she got an idea, a wild and crazy idea, but one that could pay great dividends to many people if it all worked out as she hoped.

"I need a favor, Henry.  It won't take long, but it's very important to me.  You know I've been working at that hospital outside of town.  I left some supplies there that I need for John.  Would you be so kind as to swing by and let me gather my things before dinner?  I really don't want to go there after dark." She knew he wouldn't refuse her, but she needed to not seem over-anxious either.

"Of course, Helen.  It really isn't all that far away from where we're heading.  I'll just take the road down by the depot and we'll be there in no time." He smiled and gave her a pat on the hand.  He enjoyed pleasing this fine young woman.

It was just under a half a mile to the hospital, and Helen seemed quieter than usual, enjoying the cool evening air, and the presence of the General there beside her. His presence made things a lot more comfortable. They pulled up in front of the main door of the hospital, and Stronton came around to help Helen down.

"Just wait right here, Henry, I won't be a minute." A light rain had started to fall, and there was no one outside of the building as she went in. Two minutes later she came back out the door and surprised Stronton, as she asked him to come back inside with her, saying that she needed help with something. He walked in through the door, following Helen into the main hall, and was immediately greeted with words he had not heard in over a year.

"Ten-hut!" As one, sixty men came to attention, in any manner that they could, every man saluting, honoring the great Brigadier General, in a show of respect and honor which was extended with the deepest sincerity.

Stronton was stunned by the greeting, and recovering himself from the unexpected welcome, removed his hat and lifted his hand in salute, a tear forming in his eyes. At once there was a deafening chorus of the "rebel yell", which had sent terror down the spine of many a Union soldier throughout the course of the war.

"These men want to greet you in person, Henry. Please, dinner can wait." And so the General made his rounds, all the way around the hospital, visiting with each soldier, hearing their stories, giving encouragement, with something meaningful to say to each and every man. They all knew Doctor Helen, and had nothing but the highest level of respect for her work, and her uplifting nature. She stood beside the General, telling him the names of those men who were unable to speak because of their wounds.  The walk ended at the beds of two soldiers, men who were not aware of the General's presence, men whose wounds would never heal.

Silence fell upon the room as the General led the men in prayer for these two men, asking for blessings for them and their families.  Stronton spoke at last.

"Men, I did not know that you were here.  All of Virginia is in your debt.  I promise that you will not be forgotten, and I will work to raise support for your care.  If you will have me, it would please me to come back and visit with you again sometime soon." Once again tears had found their way to the corner of his eyes. This had been an overwhelming experience, a moment of memories, a moment of regret.  Cheers rose up again as the General waved his goodbye, and led Helen to the carriage.

On the way home, Stronton had to give disappointing news to Helen.

"I'm sorry, Helen, but it looks as though I've stayed a bit too long for us to make it to the restaurant in time for dinner tonight.  Please forgive me."  His voice was quiet and reserved, the words finding it hard to leave his mouth as he spoke, still moved by his recent experience.  Helen put her arm around his, so very proud of this wonderful man, and wanting to make him very aware of just how she felt about things.

"The healing I saw there today was more wonderful than any meal I could possibly have eaten this evening.  Your being there meant everything to those men.  They need the same kind of example and leadership now as they did when you led them into battle.  Their war is not yet over, and I thank you for all that you did for them tonight."  She put her head on his shoulder, and held his arm a little bit tighter than before.

"Why didn't you tell me you were working with veterans at that hospital? Helen smiled at his question, the evening working out far better than she had planned.

"I just did."

The next morning Henry Stronton kept his appointment at the Constable's office, responding to a request from the day before. He was warmly welcomed and made to feel comfortable. The Constable spoke with admiration.

"General, it is good to see you again, and I hope you and yours are doing well. This will only take a few minutes, just so I can wrap up my investigation on the series of shootings and beatings that happened in our fair Richmond just within these last few days."

"I have here written depositions from the two witnesses who were present in the park when the shootings took place. Could you tell me, sir, what brought you to be in the park that day and at that time?" The Constable held the General in great esteem, as did most all of Virginia. But a rash of deaths coming one upon the other demanded a detailed explanation.

"I was there at the park meeting an old family friend, Mr. John Cummins, who has been a guest in my home more than once. We had happened upon one another quite by accident earlier in the day, and planned to spend time together later on, catching up on old times." So far, everything he had said was true, to a point.

"From what I understand, Mr. Cummins was shot by a lone gunman, who you then shot in turn. Can you give me more details?"

"I had seen John from a distance, and was walking toward him, when another man moved up in front of me, and fired two shots into John, and at close range. I moved in quickly, horrified by what I had seen. I drew my pistol, and shouted to him, hoping to get him to drop his weapon. Instead he turned and lifted his pistol against me, and I shot him down. I then had my man, Xander carry our friend to a nearby rooming house and sought out medical help. Fortunately, Dr. Williams was shopping nearby at the time, and I was able to get her to John's bedside very quickly. I thank Providence for grace in this matter."

"How is Mr. Cummins doing?" The Constable had put down his pen for the moment, sincerity in his concern for the General's friend.

"Doctor Williams is a magician. John Cummins was up and eating breakfast this morning when I left to visit with you here. He couldn't have been in better hands." The matter was finished, but the Constable had one last question.

"Tell me General, do you have any idea who the man was who shot your friend, or any idea as to his motive?" Stronton gave that some thought, and then answered the question the best way he could, bending the facts---just a little.

"The man who fell in the park was the notorious outlaw Rue French. I know this for a fact, because Rue French had actually come by our home days before. He was looking for the wanted criminal Jacob McPhearson, who had at one time lived there at the farm following the death of his step brother's wife, God rest her soul. Knowing the kind of man that he was, I reacted quickly to his threat toward me, understanding his willingness to murder without concern for his victims. I can only assume that his motive was money, as he was a known thief as well as a killer." Once again the General had told the truth, but with a bit of a diversion as to which man was who.

"Then Rue French it will be, and I'm sure the folks up north will be glad to hear of his passing. By the way, the Army seems to have wiped out the better part of Jacques Benine's gang which was operating back in the hills. In fact several more of his followers, were found dead in a vacant building on the same day as the shooting at the park. Jacques is still at large."

"We'll be on the lookout. Good work on your part here my friend, and let me know if there is anything else I can do to help. Good day." The men stood again and shook hands, promising to get together for lunch the next time Stronton was in town. Just as Stronton was about to leave, he turned, and went back to his old friend with a special request.

"That French fellow, the one I was forced to shoot, he was no friend of mine, but I think there will be a lot of folks who will be relieved to hear of his passing. Would it be too much to have a marker made up, just painted oak mind you, to let whoever passes by know that the world is a little bit safer now that Rue French is gone." The General then laid a gold coin down on the desk, ironically, one of the many that he had swindled from Judge Bennet on that pivotal day, a day that now seemed so long ago. Taking the pen in hand, Stronton wrote the epitaph that he had in mind on a piece of scrap paper. The Constable smiled as he read it, understanding the power of the words Stronton had written.

"It'll be just as you ask, my friend."

A short distance away, another inquiry into the events of recent days was well under way, with a young Lieutenant being questioned.

"Lieutenant Tresser, please understand that this is not a formal proceeding, but rather merely a fact finding mission. You will not be sworn in today, but just the same, we expect your responses to be complete, accurate, and to the point. Do you understand?"

"Yes, sir." And yes, he did. Notes were not being taken at this meeting. Whatever was said here this day could easily be denied. It was a set up.

"It is reported that the stolen horse and uniform of Major Winston Benedict were discovered in your tent on the evening of the day in question. Can you explain for us here how they came to be in your tent?"

"To clarify the record sir, the uniform was in the tent, neatly folded, but the horse was outside, but nearby. The uniform came into the camp a week earlier, worn by a man we knew as Major Crittendon. He was riding that same horse when he arrived. He took command upon arrival."

"Is it your habit, Lieutenant, to hand over command to any man wearing a senior officer's uniform who shows up at your camp?" The Union General was doing his best to agitate his junior.

"It is my duty to follow the orders of any senior officer at any time, sir. Major Crittendon handed me his written orders upon arrival, and I had no reason to question them. They bore your signature and seal sir."

"Do you have those orders with you Lieutenant?" This would be worth seeing, and might unlock the puzzle before them. He handed them over. They were passed around to the other committee members.

"We will hold these orders for future consideration. It is a very serious matter indeed that there is here the possibility that a complete stranger, an impostor, could have so easily infiltrated our command, and led our troops into battle, without someone questioning his identity." The Union General was posturing here, trying to find someplace to hang the blame.

"Yes sir, it is very much a matter for concern. It would be a very bad thing if our men found themselves questioning the authority of rank, especially in the presence of an enemy. However, this man's habits, knowledge, and familiarity with Army methods and terminology gave no indication that he was anything but the real deal. He knew his stuff." One of the other Union officers, a Colonel, spoke up as the interview was coming to a close.

"Lieutenant, off the record, is there anything you would like to add to these proceedings, any personal comments or observations, that we might better understand what has happened here?" The Colonel's tone was sincere and supportive. He knew very well what kind of officer the Lieutenant was, and would have nothing to do with anyone railroading a man for doing his job.

"Yes sir, and with all due respect, I served with this Major for the better part of a week, and fought in three separate engagements. Each raid was completely successful, brilliantly planned, and executed with precision. Not one of our men even got so much as a scratch, while casualties on our enemies were nearly one hundred per cent. Impostor or not, I'm here to tell you that Major Crittendon was the best damned officer I've ever served with, anytime, anywhere."

And with that, the Lieutenant was dismissed with thanks from the panel of inquiry, he being the last of the men to be interviewed. It would be much more difficult from here on out for the General.

"We can't very well punish a man for following orders here, can we? This whole thing is a mess of scrambled skunks, and we'd best be putting an end to it as soon as possible." As the ranking officer in the room, the General had the most to lose or gain here, depending on how this matter was settled. The Colonel spoke up, as he had during the proceeding. He had an idea.

"We are all aware of the political connections Major Benedict enjoys in the halls of Washington. It is important that we find a way to pull him out of his own muck here and let him and his uniform shine like gold. Any suggestions?" The three men sat in silence until the Captain, the junior officer in this room of higher ups, made a suggestion that the others couldn't.

"It seems that Major Benedict's uniform and horse were present at the raids to which the Lieutenant was referring. To my knowledge, the Lieutenant has never met Major Benedict, who may well have been using an assumed name to cover his brilliant scheme to rid the highlands of this sinister rabble. His leaving his horse and uniform behind was most likely a ruse to cover his identity, so as to maintain his well-established modesty in such things. And of course, you General sir, did indeed issue these orders, in secret, as the entire highly successful operation was planned by you from the beginning, a stroke of genius, I might add." The men in the room mulled over the opportunity the Captain's take on the matter provided.

"And so then, what shall we do with the other parties involved? Sooner or later the cat will crawl out of the bag and we'll have congress down here asking questions." The General had a point, but the Colonel had the solution.

"We'll decorate Major Benedict as a hero, giving him total credit for his part in this brilliant operation. Then we'll ship him off to Washington to speak on behalf of the War Department to try to raise additional revenue for our cause. Lieutenant Tresser and his command, along with the courier, will be given a unit citation, and then be shipped out west to help deal with the Indian menace. And you, General, might just get that second star as a result of all of this." The room became quiet once again, with knowing smiles all around, the matter having been settled.

Turning difficulty into opportunity is the hallmark of inspired leadership.

# CHAPTER THIRTY-FOUR

John Cummins' recovery was going very well, in fact Dr. Helen Williams was almost ready to send him back to Dellmont to continue his recovery --- almost.

She had a deep and troubling concern, one she had kept to herself until now. She shared her feelings with the General, a man she had come to trust with any secrets or feelings she might have.

"Henry, John Cummins is well enough to return to your farm to finish his healing. I'm just not sure it's such a good idea to take him back there with you. There are some things that might fester up and re-appear out of nowhere. I'm very concerned." The General gave her his well-known disapproving stare, all in fun, and thought it all pishposh.

"Ginny has been doting over this man ever since she got here. In fact, except for your coming in and checking on him from time to time, she's been guarding him like a mother hen. None of the rest of us can hardly get in to speak to him."

"That's right. And there's a reason. As best as I can tell, he doesn't seem to realize that he has lived another life, another identity. We've been careful not to bring the matter up, but sooner or later a tongue will slip. John Cummins does not seem to remember that he was ever known as Rue French, or of any of the things he did as an outlaw before he was shot. But it's patchwork. He seems to remember many things, including his visit with you at Dellmont. But he doesn't remember the bad things. In fact, he thinks that Ginny is his wife." Those last words sank in. The General sat back and gave that some thought. He had seen the long term effects of battle shock before. Men had gone mad, unable to recognize their own families.

"So if I understand it right, you feel that someday someone will slip and say something about Rue French, or maybe even come forward, identifying him as Rue French, and it all might come back to him, and in a very bad way." The General saw the wisdom of ages in Helen's eyes, and had come to understand what a strong woman she was.

"Or worse. He might lash out at those around him, falling under a kind of trance, reliving his past and the violence he knew so well. I met this man when he was still very much the outlaw we knew him to be. He was faking amnesia then to try to squirm out of two counts of murder and one count of horse thievery. This man was very, very good---an accomplished actor. If I hadn't seen him when he was acting before, I might think he was doing it again. But not this time. This is for real. The man lying on that bed is not the same man I first met back in Pennsylvania."

"Is he really that different? Can a gunshot wound to the head really change the makeup of a man that much?" Stronton was out of his depth here.

"I'm not sure. But remember, he has suffered two serious head wounds in little more than a month's time. Amazingly, the man we see here today is actually very much like the man who saved my life that day at the farm. He's a wonderful fellow. I'm just concerned as to where the other one went, and what happens if he comes back."

They sat together for a while then, holding hands in the quiet morning air. A blue jay was busy complaining to his neighbors about something or other. It seems that everyone has something to worry about, even birds.

Laughter could be heard coming through the open door, as John and Ginny delighted over some humorous poetry she had read aloud. It was very funny, and it was John's turn to read the next page.

John was up and around now, five minutes every hour, and his color was much improved. The wound on his head was still seeping a bit, and he wouldn't be able to wear a hat for a while, but the dizziness was mostly gone, and walking was becoming easier again. He'd be giving up his cane by the end of the week.

Helen heard the laughter as she came into the room, and enjoyed the love that she saw between them. Ginny was quite a girl. John Cummins was a very lucky man. But Helen knew how tragically that all could change. It was time for another heart to heart with Miss Stronton.

"Ginny, I hate to pull you away from our patient, but there are a few things I need to speak to you about concerning his care and feeding after I'm gone." Gone? This all sounded rather strange to Ginny, knowing how close Helen and her father had become in the last many days. She knew there had to be more to it. But with a smile and a kiss on John's cheek, Ginny followed Helen once again into the room across the hall. Something was wrong.

"What's this all about, Helen? Is there something here I don't see? Daddy and I agree that he's well enough to go back to Dellmont, and you said so yourself. And where are you going that you won't be around for his 'care and feeding'? What do you mean?" Ginny was speaking right up here. She and Helen had grown quite close, and Ginny had even been sleeping in Helen's room at night.

"John is doing very well, and you're right, he's ready to go. I spoke with your father earlier and shared my concerns with him, just as I will share my concerns with you now. You and I both knew this man when he was Rue French, dashing, daring, and very dangerous. I've been listening, and John seems to have no recollection of that identity, or of his history as a gunman and a thief. My concern is what happens if suddenly that all comes back to him? How might he react to those around him? The 'what if' is scarier than the 'what is'." Helen was surprised by the reaction she got now from young Ginny. The quiet calmness in the girl's eyes changed the light in the room. Things became suddenly different.

"He hasn't forgotten, not at all. Rue French was his own creation, made to deal with the loss of his wife, Priscilla. That's really what this has all been about, a betrayal by a beautiful woman, to a man who was too pure to understand the evil she represented. You may have listened, but you haven't heard everything. He and I have talked about Rue French, and the things that happened to him, and Judge Bennet, and the things he did to me. We've been dealing with these things the whole time, often at night, when everyone else is asleep, when I tiptoe back into his room. I can be very quiet when I want to be." They both smiled at that, Ginny being known for her giggles, and humming her songs. Who would have thought that girl could ever be quiet?

"But Ginny, he thinks you're his wife!" Helen wasn't ready to write her concerns off so soon. Intimacy can hide insecurities.

"I am his wife, Helen, in every way but the ceremony. A piece of paper will never make a marriage, or even vows if they're spoken just to get the ceremony over with. No, I'll have a proper wedding, and you will stand with me. And I fully expect to be standing with you when you marry my father. But remember, I intend to think of you as my sister, not my mother." Helen cackled like a hen at that, realizing how wonderful life was about to become for the two of them, and just how blessed the two of them were.

The giggling and laughing became nearly hysterical when Ginny mentioned that she would be walking down the aisle with her father twice---once for him to give her away to John, and once for her to give him away to Helen. The moment was priceless, and then it was over.

The air was shattered as four shots were fired, one upon the other. Those shots had come from John's room. The women shared a glance of disbelief and horror, and ran through the door, the unthinkable becoming real.

# CHAPTER THIRTY-FIVE

There are many things that a doctor can do to save their patient's life. Medicines, surgeries, ointments, heat, ice, and even leeches can all be used to help restore a sick man back to health.

It can even be as simple as the timely moving of a patient's bed.

Cummins had complained for two days about the confine ment he felt from not being able to look out the window of his room. Hours upon hours of staring at the wallpapered surroundings was much too foreign for him to live with. That morning his friends had finally given in, and after first getting him safely to the chair, worked together to move the heavy bed over by the window overlooking the street beyond. There was a tree nearby, with berries on it that kept the birds coming and going all day long. It was a welcome relief from the monotony.

Still, Cummins didn't look out the window all of the time, especially not while his lovely Ginny was there to occupy his hours, which was often.  But she had gone with Helen into a room across the hall for a few moments of girl talk, leaving him alone and unattended.  He looked out the window now, wishing he were outside, enjoying the sun on his face once again.  His eyes felt heavy and tired as he took in the view, the tree, the birds, the street beyond.  But sometimes what we don't see is more important that what we do see.

It had only been a glimpse, a fleeting shadow, but the image was certain, and the danger it brought with it could not be mistaken.  He had only seconds.

Cummins moved quickly, at least as quickly as he could, crawling off the bed, and lunging for the soft cushioned chair beyond.  Next to that chair was Helen's leather bag. He grasped it just as a man in dark clothing rushed into the room, gun in hand, hatred in his eyes.

No words were exchanged, no challenge given. None were needed.  Four shots were fired, shots which spelled death, and loss, the waste of high and mighty intentions gone awry.

Across the hall the two women froze in place for only an instant, and then ran for the door, heedless of the danger that could be waiting for them there.

Helen screamed as they ran into the room, finding a bloodstained body laying prone across the bed, dressed in dark clothing, with an unused pistol still in his hand.  On the floor near the chair sat John Cummins holding Helen's .44 at the ready, watching his attacker for any remaining signs of life.

But Jacques Benine's life had already ended, his dreams of glory and greatness dying along with his legacy of evil and bondage. Sellah had known it all along --- he had chosen the wrong chicken.

Other boarders at the rooming house had converged quickly, guns in hand, ready to do battle as needed, though not yet knowing what all the shooting was about. Cummins made the necessary introduction.

"Thanks for coming down to visit folks. And allow me to introduce my guest to you. Over there is none other than the notorious Jacques Benine, murderer, thief, and slave runner."

After assessing the situation, and the carnage which had invaded his place of business, it was the landlord himself who put the proper words to the moment, not knowing the irony of what he had said.

"Mr. Cummins, I have decided that you are now well enough to leave, and I expect you to be gone by morning. Any man who attracts bullets the way you do is not safe to be around." There could be no argument there.

But this episode had a happy and profitable ending for the landlord after all. For years to come, and as the story of the shootings grew, that room would be rented out for three times the going rate, as folks came to wallow in the history of the place, and gaze at Helen's bullet hole which still to this day can be seen in the wall over by that same bed.

# CHAPTER THIRTY-SIX

The air was surprisingly warm for autumn as beautiful red and orange clouds announced the morning that next day. Birds sang in a chorus of busyness, as the world awakened anew, life springing from decay, day turning away the night.

John and Ginny had the carriage all to themselves this time, beginning their life together, traveling this day back to Dellmont, the place they would now call home. The special bond which held them together would be made stronger by the darkness their lives had overcome. Their need for happiness would cast aside the kind of pettiness which consumes so many other couples' lives.

The General had decided to stay behind for now, enjoying his daily visits with the men at the hospital, and working diligently to organize his many friends and fellow officers in an effort to provide for those wounded heroes, many whom would never again be able to provide for themselves. Still, every effort would be made to find them work, an honest living, giving them a chance to hold their heads high again.

On the way out of town, Ginny asked John to turn off onto a side road, following a hand drawn map that her father had given her the night before. He said he had been speaking with the Constable that evening, and had come across some information that he thought might be useful to Ginny, or Cummins, or both.

The side road led to an old cemetery, mostly overgrown with neglect, but with a newer portion where the soil had been more recently turned. The map indicated a spot where the paupers' graves were laid, a final resting place for those who had no one to speak for them, the unknown, and the uncared for.

But there a new wooden marker, painted white with black letters stood alone, seeming to glow a lovely shade of red, facing the east as it did, and catching the final rays of the morning sun before it continued its journey through the autumn sky.

John Cummins stood there with his wife-to-be, and gazed down upon that marker, its four words telling a truth as powerful as death itself. They shared an embrace, and a kiss for luck, their old lives now behind them. Here then was closure.

The four words on the marker read as follows:

RUE FRENCH
IS
DEAD

And thus the small town Sheriff inherited a part of Rue French's legacy after all, his name, a $10.000 plot of Virginia soil, and a splendid marker, paid for with a piece of stolen gold.

And now John Cummins could live his life in peace and prosperity, with his lovely Ginny by his side, away from the torment and fears of the past, a golden future awaiting them together.

If only it could have been that easy.

THE END --- for now.

.

www.ingramcontent.com/pod-product-compliance
Lightning Source LLC
Chambersburg PA
CBHW070610130626
46556CB00001B/326